LADY VENGEANCE

KATHERINE BONE

DEDICATION

To all the girls who never got asked to prom.

PROLOGUE

*K*ingston-upon-Thames, Surrey, 1814

"You missed."

"I rarely miss," Lady Lora Hawkesbury countered. Hawkesburys seldom blundered, but her brother Nicholas, the Earl of Norbiton, enjoyed testing her patience.

"Could it be that your luck has run its course?"

"Shake a cloth in the wind!" If she didn't love her brother immensely, she might have given him a sound thrashing. Although, it was not in her demeanor to quarrel. Witty banter was a staple of giddy glee and the bread of life, also a result of their highly competitive natures, and assurance that she wasn't like other young women with sugary sap flowing through their veins, sickening sycophants who wasted the prime of bloom dreaming of balls and parties. "Continue to bray like a donkey, Nicholas. I will make my own luck."

Indeed, a will of iron coursed through Lora's veins, filling her with a determination to excel in sport and intellectual pursuits that were denied to proper young women schooled to run households. Target shooting and the exhilaration of a pleasant ride across an open meadow fueled her spirit. Papa had encouraged her, allowing her to ride astride and to come and go at will, especially because she didn't have a mother to constrict those activities. In fact, it could be said that her father doted on her, failing to differentiate between the sexes. He'd taught her skills—she was informed—that would never benefit a lady of the *ton* or win her a prospective husband.

Pshaw. What did she need a husband for? She had Papa and Nicholas. She lived in a large country house with plenty of farmland, tenants, and beauty to sustain her passions. And while their father was currently recovering from a hunting accident, Papa still encouraged them to go on hunting expeditions into the wild, declaring himself the happiest of men as he watched them ride off together.

"Father taught you well," Nicholas said. "But I have more years on you, sprite. More practice. Patience. Which means I have got more training."

His taunt only fueled her desire to win their five-pound bet. "Bah!" She laughed. "The only thing you have achieved that I cannot aspire to is you are a marquess-in-waiting. Which reminds me. Were you not equally taught to do the honorable thing—and at all times—in the presence of a lady?"

He harrumphed. "Lady? Show me the lady and—"

"Concede," she said, forbidding him to mock her. "I won this round."

"I never yield." A truth universally acknowledged as he was one of the most formidable young men in the district, and much sought after by the female sex. His sharp mind and exceptional morals promised compassion and constancy. She could not help but admire him as he turned to stare at her.

Sunlight glinted off his handsome face and green eyes. "But, when it comes to you, I am defenseless." He widened his arms. "I rebuke the orders of Society. And, were it possible, I would restructure the whole of it for you. But as with any hunt, there are expectations, strategies in place. For you. For me. And Father's accident hastens the trajectory of the inevitable beat of the drum. Unless he recovers, I will have to take his place. And when I do, expectations will be harder to ignore."

"Yes. I know," she said, admiring his integrity all the more as he sat tall and lithe in the saddle. They were both determined to carry on their father's legacy, come what may, haunted by possibilities and the ramifications of what-ifs. "Anticipation rules many a heart, but I know you will never abandon me. You are good and honorable." Warmth of the moment filled her and she beamed. "Papa's doing."

Their bond was strong, her brother's bluntness his most admirable trait. True power came from honesty. Truth buckled the knees of lofty men and prospective suitors in pursuit of weighty dowries. Verity protected women from letches who haunted ballrooms in search of easy prey, while civility protected them from scandal and gossip. In turn, courtesy recommended both men and women alike, and Nicholas rose above them all. He would never desert or enslave her to a man she did not love and respect. That fact sustained her.

"He taught us well. Life is a game, and Society does not play fair."

"Then you and I must strive to change the system," Nicholas said, smiling.

The futility of it all pitched in her stomach. How did one alter the path of the stars or the course of the moon? "You cannot defeat a charging bull."

"No," he said, gazing off in the direction of their estate

house—Winterbourne. "We cannot hold back the hands of time, though many try. No." He shook his head and met her stare, a strange look transforming his face. "There is only one constant in life, Lora. Change. And it will come to us whether or not we desire it. We cannot keep the world at bay for long."

She tsked. "That is easy for you to say. If anything happens to Papa, you will take his place, and I . . ." A ridiculous solution entered her mind. "I will enter a convent and provide sustenance for hungry nuns."

Nicholas burst out laughing. "We're not Catholic."

"You are right," she said with a straight face. A dark harbinger of doom settled over her. Few opportunities were in a woman's favor, other than marriage, a position as a governess, or becoming a doting aunt. Therefore, she had decided not to marry unless a man proved himself worthy. That disqualified their cousin, Samuel. The barbaric man was determined to make her his. "But no battle has ever been won without alteration."

"*If you know neither the enemy nor yourself, you will succumb in every battle.*"

"And there you have it." She giggled softly. "You forget that I have studied Sun Tzu and understand exactly what to do. If I cannot join a convent because I am not Catholic, I will simply have to convert."

"You will do nothing of the sort."

"Whyever not?"

"I do not need to give you a history lesson. Catholics face the challenge of existing without prejudice in a modern world, being forced to worship in secret. No, indeed. Converting will only submerge you into deeper depths." He singled out a target and raised his bow, nocking an arrow and stretching back the string until the shaft kissed his cheek. Like Robin Hood of old, he was magnificent, posing before her, muscular, majestic, and magical, his profile a delight to behold before he let loose. After a moment's hesitation, he exclaimed, "Bullseye!"

"Are you certain?" She peered into the wood to verify he'd hit the mark. "I think your arrow hit to the left of mine."

"Oh, Lora," he said, ignoring her taunt. "This is the moment, isn't it? The two of us. Riding together just like we did when we were children, racing and laughing, a fire in our bellies and our blood boiling to be the best."

"Truly." She nocked an arrow in one swift motion and let it fly, knowing no other enjoyment than being by her brother's side. Nicholas lifted her spirits. His assurances and companionship had kept her going since Papa's accident. "This is all that I live and breathe for. If moments like these could go on forever, I should be the happiest of women."

"I do desire for you to be happy, Lora." His current seriousness fled when he added jovially, "But opportunity begs me to inform you that you missed again."

"Impossible!" Making a show of it, she rose in the saddle and peered through the trees, pouting playfully. "How can you tell?"

"It is the way of things," he responded drily. "Men are far superior to women, you know."

"I do not! In fact, I distinctly heard *your* arrow hit to the left of mine and fall haplessly to the forest floor. Was that not the crackle of defeat disturbing our serenity?"

"No." His dubious laughter highlighted the absurdity of her statement, even though she had heard something in the wood. "Come. There is no better time than now to find out who is the better shot."

Kicking in his heels, he set off for the trees, leaving her gawking at his mount's hindquarters. Determined not to be second best, she slapped the reins and followed. "Gee up!"

The great black beneath her bolted, its swift hooves and her light weight heightening her chances of catching him up.

"Isn't it time to admit defeat, brother?" she shouted. "Admit it. I am a much better shot."

He glanced back over his shoulder, egging her on. "On. What. Day?"

Two-hundred yards. One-hundred-and-fifty yards. She was almost upon him.

Then, contrary to anything she comprehended, Nicholas arched, whipping back in his saddle unnaturally, seizing. The rush of excitement filling her lungs instantly congealed, and her world capsized as her brother slipped from the saddle to the cold, inflexible earth.

"Nicholas?" Heart pounding wildly, she raced to him, dismounting before her horse came to a stop. She sprinted to his side, skidding to the ground beside him. Nightmarish images of her father's hunting accident flashed before her eyes as she carefully turned him over. The motion brought her up short when she stared at a short, well-placed bolt from a crossbow sticking out of his heart. His former jubilance reverberated between her ears. *'Bullseye!'* A violent sob wracked her body. "Nicholas!"

Death deafened her cry. His clear green eyes stared blankly skyward, the severe turn of his lips deforming his once happy mouth.

"No!" She gripped his shoulders. "This cannot be!" She shook him to rouse him back to life. *No. No. No.* "Don't go. Don't leave me! Not now. Not yet!"

But nothing could be done. Nicholas was dead.

How?

Sanity returned as the reality of what had just happened slapped her in the face. Someone had murdered her brother right before her eyes! Slowly, she lowered his shoulders and reached behind her for an arrow. Nocking her bow, she searched the wood line, conscious that a dark veil of hatred and vengeance had descended over her, a hate so deep it sentenced any notion of convents into hellish oblivion.

Warily, she watched and waited for a sound, a movement.

Birdsong quieted and wind whistled through the trees, the breeze ruffling the feather in her bonnet, tickling her cheek. And then she heard it, the sound of feet shuffling through the underbrush.

There! A man stopped every few feet to peer at the carnage. Their eyes locked, and in that instant, she let loose, targeting the orange cloth about the man's neck, the color distinct and completely foreign to the winter terrain. But Nicholas's murderer anticipated her actions, easily avoiding the shaft, which sank unpardonably into the tree trunk where he'd stood seconds before. She withdrew another arrow from her quiver and aimed again.

The man taunted her, aiming his crossbow, then laughed maniacally before slipping away.

"I will find you!" An unrecognizable shriek of anguish possessed her, taking her by surprise. She looked down at Nicholas and stared at his unseeing eyes, sinking to the earth to cradle his limp form, this new reality, so foreign and foul, branding her brain. "No matter what it takes. No matter how long." Tears coursed down her cheeks, inexplicable loss and sadness marring what was, what would be. "I will hunt down your murderer and make him pay. No path will be too long, no deprivation too great. So help me, God."

CHAPTER 1

Physical excellence does not of itself produce a good mind and character: on the other hand, excellence of mind and character will make the best of the physique it is given.

~ Plato

Mayfair, late July 1815

"STAND AND DELIVER!"

"Stand and deliver?" Did anyone rob men at gunpoint on rural roads anymore? Intrigued, Myles Rutland, Duke of Beresford, regarded the man before him with a frown, disbelieving this odd tale of woe.

"That's what the blackguard said."

"If you were traveling in a mail coach, address your accusations to the Postmaster and High Constable." The last man guilty of highway robbery was hung in Hempstead in 1802, after a recognizable loose girth-strap and a chance encounter with a post-boy in the Marlborough Forest.

"I was traveling in a private coach, on your land, I might add, Your Grace."

"My land?" *Devil take me!* That was a horse of a different color. "Did you recognize this highwayman?"

"Highwayman?" His fanatical laughter filled the room, suggesting that the man might be unhinged. "I never said my attacker was a man."

Myles tensed. What else was the man implying—trolls? "Grimes, is it?"

"Lucas Grimes, Esquire, at your service, Your Grace."

"Did I, or did I not, distinctly hear you say that a blackguard on the London Road attacked you?"

"Yes, Your Grace."

"Then explain yourself," he said, beginning to lose patience. He was late to another one of Lady Jersey's soirees. *Damn my eyes!*

"Forgive me, Your Grace. What you ask is not a simple thing for a man to confess." Grimes inspected his shabby appearance, frowning, then made a show of straightening his cuffs. "If I had been to a tavern, deep into my cups, perhaps I would call into question what my own eyes and ears saw and heard, but I did see her. A man does not expect to fall prey—"

"To confirm." He raised his hand to interrupt the man as it suddenly occurred to him that if Grimes wasn't accusing a man for the offenses against him, it could only mean—Peppered with confusion, he asked, "Are you implying that a *woman* robbed you at gunpoint?"

"Gunpoint?" The solicitor's eyes shot up. "I never

mentioned such a weapon, though she wore a brace of very handsome pistols."

Absurd! He'd never heard of such a woman. "If she did not use her pistols, how on earth did she manage to frighten you into submission?"

"I never said I submitted."

Curse the man for talking in circles. "You said you were —" The man's incoherent mumbling finally cut through the last of Myles's patience. "I couldn't quite hear that."

"Your Grace." The man leaned forward, eyes widening. "She expertly wielded a bow and arrow."

First, a marauding woman, now this? Were his ears deceiving him? *Preposterous!* He sat back, almost too stunned to speak. But, of course, the truth was obvious to him now. Darkness of night, urgency of sound, danger, and fear. Circumstances like these influenced people to believe the oddest things. "This is not the Middle Ages, Mr. Grimes."

"Do you doubt my word, Your Grace? In case you have not heard, solicitors take particular care to avoid mincing words."

Myles leaned forward, feeling a novel tug at the man's entreaty. "A woman, you say? Expertly wielding a bow and arrow?"

Grimes nodded, albeit slowly, making him wonder if the man was providing the entire truth. Perhaps he had invented the tale to offset any embarrassment for the damage to his *articles*.

"And you expect that to counter my disbelief?"

"Your Grace, I assure you, I am not playing you false." Grimes waved his arms, the awkward motion hinting at barely held composure. "I have journeyed far to plead my case, have I not? And at great expense to myself."

Grimes had a point, though he hadn't quite got to it yet. "Perhaps you experienced a trick of moonlight—"

"Do not let these spectacles deceive you, Your Grace. I see everything clearly."

"And no one came to your defense? Your driver? Postillion? Without witnesses to verify—"

"They abandoned me to my fate. You have my word as a gentleman!"

"Be that as it may, the law requires proof. If events happened as you described and a highwaywoman robbed you but you suffered no—"

"Harm?" The man lunged forward, disturbing several objects on the desk between them, his zeal to be believed testing the last constraints of Myles's patience.

He glared at Grimes, but allowed the man his say.

"I am familiar with the rumble and harry of the opposite sex and can tell a woman from a man without the help of a full moon. You must allow me to clarify the damage done to my pride. For it is great, I assure you."

"Go on."

Grimes grimaced. "It is imperative for you to know that I have never met a more cunning, cold, and convincing individual. Indeed, I shall go to my grave with her image branded into the depths of my soul." He lifted his hands from the desk and straightened to his full height, which, for a portly man, provided little more elevation. "Heed my warning. We must hunt down, capture, and punish this woman. She is a pillory for anyone traveling on the London Road through Kingston-upon-Thames."

"You weave a fascinating tale. And while I understand your frustration and agree that something must be done to ease your discomfort, we need evidence according to the law. Unless someone catches them in the act, the process becomes daunting. The authorities have brought no one to trial for highway robbery in Kingston for twenty years."

Jerry Abershawe's hanging aptly put a stop to that.

"My testimony alone should be enough. But if it is proof you desire, I will gladly supply it." The man began awkwardly fumbling with the fall front of his trousers.

"Grimes!" Myles bolted from his chair. "What on earth are you doing?"

"Evidence, Your Grace. You asked for it, and I shall give it to you." With that, he dropped his trousers, turned, and raised his shirttail. The shocking act revealed a three-inch wound. "*Here* is your proof."

"She shot you . . . in the arse?" Myles quickly put the stopper on his laughter. An injury like that required aim and purpose, an improbable feat at night, making him marvel at this bandit's crudeness. Grimes had mentioned the woman was cunning. The whole affair seemed too farfetched to be believed.

To witness such a woman loose an arrow like Picts of old—

Sobering quickly, another thought struck him. "If you were in your carriage, how did you receive such a blow? And why would this *she-bandit* treat you so ill?"

The man clothed himself, his hands fumbling clumsily as he worked. "She demanded that I exit my carriage."

"And?" Being an excellent judge of character, he guessed the outcome.

"And . . . when I refused, out of an obligation to protect my client's goods, she shot an arrow between my legs. Entirely too close to my . . . Well, you get the idea."

Myles blinked. "While you were seated in the carriage?"

"Yes, Your Grace. It all happened so fast, I had no time to react. I confess, my life passed before my eyes, including—but not limited to—the children I might not produce."

Confounding. "What did you do next?"

"What else could I do?" Grimes harrumphed. "I carefully extracted myself from the carriage and decided to—"

"Run." The scene became clear now. This time, he didn't fight the laughter bubbling up in his chest, furthering Grimes' humiliation. Sitting down, he tented his fingers beneath his nose, struggling for composure.

"Yes." Grimes spat. "I admit it, I ran. It seemed the only solution at the time. She was on horseback. I was on foot, the woods dark and thick. I misjudged her. Everything happened so fast. I—"

"Why not just give her what she asked for?" Myles lowered his hands, his mind reaching for something he could not quite grasp. The highwaywoman's cold-blooded determination drew him in, making him wonder what would drive a female to break the law. "What were her demands? Be specific. Any information you provide will be crucial to your case."

The man smiled for the first time since entering Myles's office. "You will investigate the incident then?"

"Since this *incident* took place on my land, I suppose it is my duty to look into it."

Though it was little consolation that he'd spent insufficient enough time in Surrey before and after his father's death, news of this hoyden's activities motivated him. Yes. If Grimes was telling the truth—and thus far, Myles had little reason to suspect otherwise—returning to Kingston would provide a diversion from seeds of division, military aggression, and debates of treaties and declarations. The trip might also provide an opportunity to become reacquainted with Lady Lora Putney. To his knowledge, she hadn't been to London since her first season. Perhaps it was time to discover why. Lord knew he needed a distraction from matchmaking mamas eager to attach their daughters to an eligible duke.

As the current Duke of Beresford, he'd quashed demons of loss and suffocating regret to support the Crown. He'd devoted himself to the House of Lords, where they debated alternatives to the long series of years that were destroying the United Kingdom's hopes of tranquility. In particular, he'd winnowed through unfounded opinions, groundless prejudices, and erroneous information, while Wellington had trounced Bonaparte, a man who supported neither peace nor truce, on the 18th of June. And yet, discord continued. Lord Grey and Robert Wilson misreported a French victory to a packed house at Brook's, and Samuel Whitbread, a great admirer of Napoleon, upon learning the truth, committed suicide. As a consequence, the triumph many declared a *'ray of sunshine'* could not last.

In Earl Bathurst's words: *'If a government exercised its functions in a manner which was dangerous to its neighbors, those neighbors had a right to proscribe that government, if necessary.'*

Is that what Kingston needed?

What about the widows and orphans Waterloo had created? Thousands of veterans were returning to the kingdom—discharged soldiers, sailors on half-pay, and the wounded. Who would defend them? He'd neglected the market town for far too long. And what would returning cost him? He despised the city. Thieves multiplied on market streets and the wrong lot took in urchins, forcing them to survive by vim and vigor. Many were blameless because they lived in a constant, brutal hell. Now more were set to join them, driven by economic hardship.

Could Grimes's attacker simply be a city woman who'd ventured to the country for easy pickings? Perhaps a tavern wench or widow in dire straits. But where would such a female acquire the skills necessary to humiliate a solicitor on his way to a client? And, why?

"Who did you say your client was again?" he asked Grimes, who stood awkwardly before him.

"I didn't say, Your Grace. That is ... confidential."

Myles had had enough of secrecy. "Not if it pertains to your case."

"It does." The man grumbled. "I was on my way to see the Honorable Thomas Hawkesbury with several of the barrister's files."

"The Marquess of Putney's younger brother?" He hadn't interacted with the man in years. That was not an oversight on his part.

"Yes, Your Grace."

"And do the papers in your possession concern him?"

"Yes, Your Grace." Grimes cleared his throat and handed him a leatherbound satchel. "That is to say, matters pertaining to his brother's accident, the death of the marquess's son, and questions about the line of succession."

"The laws of succession are inflexible." Myles tapped the haversack, intrigued. "I recall both of these events with equal sadness."

His father had attended the funeral. But he hadn't been able to pay his respects after the young earl's death because of political debate.

He opened the pouch and perused the contents, frowning. There were ledgers listing debts paid by Thomas Hawkesbury for his son. Reckless vowels to friends, promising payment. A letter threatening the son to take the 'King's Shilling' if he did not accept a commission and discharge papers from the 33rd Regiment of Foot. *Being forced to enlist is a dire fate for an aristocrat.* What's more, there were promissory notes to moneylenders, and peculiar gambling losses at Tattersalls, Ascot, and Epsom, Gentlemen clubs and gaming hells. He furrowed his brows. "Is anything missing?"

"No, Your Grace. That is what confounds me."

"She took nothing?" *Odd.* He shook his head, baffled, then returned the solicitor's belongings. Life produced forces for good and evil. Zara's line in *The Mourning Bride,* often wrongly credited to Shakespeare, struck him. *'Heav'n has no rage, like love to hatred turn'd, nor Hell a fury like a woman scorn'd.'* "She made no other demands?"

Grimes narrowed his stare. "As I lay there bleeding, she said, 'I asked you to leave the carriage. That was all you had to do. Only the guilty run.' She stared down at me. 'I will not *miss* next time.'"

"Miss?"

"My response exactly. To prove her point, she quickly shot the hat off my head." He retrieved his headgear, a felt stovepipe hat, and stuck his fingers through the hole in the six-and-a-half-inch crown.

Myles's jaw dropped as the hole appeared to be angled dangerously close to a man's skull. "What happened next?"

Grimes tucked his folio under his arm. "She retrieved her arrow."

"From your hat?"

"Not that one."

He leaned forward in his chair, aghast. "Do you mean to say that she—"

"No. No. No, Your Grace." The solicitor shook his head gravely. "The shaft grazed my arse . . . then fortuitously buried itself into a tree stump. The threat to my person was real, however. I had the distinct impression she regretted not shooting me through."

"I see."

"Good." Grimes bowed. "I presented my case, and now that I have received assurances you will look into the matter, I shall not take up any more of your time."

"What were her conditions?" Myles blurted out, stopping the man from leaving as he gathered his belongings and headed for the door.

"Your Grace?" Grimes asked, perplexed.

"Her demands, man. What were they?"

He reluctantly returned to Myles's desk. "If her goal was to humiliate me, she triumphed."

"But she gave no further orders?" he asked, trying to mask his shock. "No reason why she detained you?"

Color flooded Grimes's cheeks, a mix of displeasure and discomfort. "She conveyed a message, Your Grace."

"Intended for whom?" His impatience was at an end.

"Hawkesbury, of course," Grimes said as if Myles couldn't keep up.

At last. "Go on."

"Revenge is best served sweet."

CHAPTER 2

*K*ingston-upon-Thames, late August 1815

"IT BEGINS."

The happy golden hues on the overstuffed damask furniture brought Lora little pleasure as she raised a steaming cup of tea to her lips. Another sleepless night had delivered her to her usual perch in the parlor window. There, pensive and poised, she daydreamed about a certain duke—as she often did without reprieve, gazing outdoors—longing to be free like birds fluttering from limb to limb in the gardens and the rotunda beyond. Creatures of the air cared nothing for fashion or manners, house parties or dances or marriage or revenge, though the weather played a significant role in their bountiful cheerfulness. A higher power had clothed each bird magnificently for what lay in store on a day-to-day basis. If only someone had shown her that same kindness. She longed to be like a bird, soaring high above the fray, able to avoid hazards with equal finesse.

This morning, however, fog and rain threatened to swallow the terrain, offering her no contentment. Like a bad omen, gloom settled over her and snuffed her spirits like a vulnerable candle in the wind, reminding her of the pain that accompanied every errand.

Grumbling with displeasure, she glanced down at her teacup. The medicinal effects of tea usually soothed her agitation. But her plans were thwarted when Miss Margaret Percival, her mother's sister, decided to open Winterbourne for guests. Aunt Meg intended to find her a suitable match, and before the summer was over. As a result, and with or without Lora's approval, a deluge of people would flood the premises, promoting goodwill and conversation, and making it nearly impossible to escape at whim.

The doors of Winterbourne would also receive her cousin, Lieutenant Samuel Hawkesbury, who had just returned from Waterloo. His long-standing animosity and burning desire to take her brother's place in the line of succession made clear he would inherit everything—and in his irrational mind, her, too.

Over my dead body.

She choked, setting her teacup down with a clatter. The very idea of Samuel assuming her father's role as the Marquess of Putney was an appalling reminder that she could not reverse time. And why shouldn't she abhor the idea? Throughout his life, Samuel's envy had influenced everything, dampening the mood, ruining family gatherings, and careening conversation into a fiery pit. Now, with Nicholas gone, the only thing standing in Samuel's way was Papa and her uncle, Thomas Hawkesbury. Once they were gone, the estate and Papa's title would subsequently fall to her cousin, polluting the halls of Winterbourne forever.

I will do whatever it takes to prevent such an outrage.

Meg cleared her throat, effectively putting an end to her ruminations.

Lora glanced at her aunt, quickly discovering that her ill-tempered musings had earned another of Meg's infamous glowers. A minor slip like this, even in private, had the potential to undo all that she'd strived so hard to achieve these many months in her pursuit of Nicholas's killer. Nervously, she picked up her teacup and saucer, the porcelain clattering in her hands.

"Is it your intention to break every tea set in this house?"

"No, Aunt. Truly. I have no notion what has come over me." *Liar!*

"Do you not?" Aunt Meg didn't seem convinced as she bent diligently to her embroidery once more.

Lora couldn't resist saying, "An impulsive female wouldn't stop at this teacup. She'd break every dish in the house if it meant a certain person would never be able to use them."

"Lora!" Meg pricked her finger and gasped, any sign of humor gone. She sucked on the digit, wincing. "I applaud your wit, my dear, but what good can come from breaking the dishes? How will we feed our guests? Think, my dear. You are too willful. I urge you to practice more diplomacy. Trust me when I say that it is never right to resort to violence. Nothing can be gained—"

"By resorting to hostility. Anger thoroughly shatters people's lives." Lora drew in a deep breath, trying not to engage, trying without fail to push her brother's death stare out of her mind. "Let us pray my cousin does not test the violence of my affections."

"Lora." Meg frowned, but Lora did not care. She meant every word because she believed Samuel's lust for Winterbourne made him somehow responsible for her brother's death. "You are my sister's only child, my pleasing, practical, philosophical niece. Since Evie's passing, we have been indulging you, if you'll allow me to say so."

Lady Evelyn, the Marchioness of Putney—Lora's mother —faded from Lora's mind with every passing year, no matter how hard she clung to the memories or stared at the portrait hanging over the mantel.

"We must all accept that your mother is gone, that Nicholas is gone, and that no one can take their place."

Unless Papa remarried and his new bride conceived a son. The jarring thought quickly rattled Lora's brain. Yes. Papa simply must recover from his injuries and marry again.

But how was that possible when his spirits were so low?

Meg swiped at an errant tear, the solemn act stirring waterworks in the backs of Lora's eyes. "Nicholas's death was tragic, as was your father's accident. Without hope for his full recovery, however, you will need a husband to provide protection. It is only fitting and right that your uncle should acquire Winterbourne in the event your father's condition takes a sudden turn, and then his son."

"Aunt!"

"The fact remains. Hawkesbury and Samuel are the rightful heirs."

Her lips curled in distaste as she placed her teacup and saucer on the side table, causing quite a clatter. "Samuel intends to marry me."

"Would that be so terrible? Happenstance, you would not have to leave Winterbourne."

She stared at Meg in horror. "He is my cousin. What's more. He's a vile, distasteful, miscreant. I want no part of him. He's a stain upon all, and—"

"Enough!"

Lora bristled at her aunt's tone.

"Harness your tongue. It does you no credit."

But Meg did not know Samuel like Lora did. She had not

been privy to his endless taunts and mean-spirited tricks. The times he'd broken expensive family heirlooms and blamed Nicholas. Or the despicable ways he'd tortured harmless animals.

Pausing and sighing, Meg studied her embroidery. "You and I were born into a world where women rarely get what they want, let alone deserve. I will not hear another word of you never marrying. My own bitter disappointment of never bearing children should be example enough, and I despair that kind of future for you, forced to rely on kind relatives." She gazed at Lora fondly. "Your father is a compassionate man. It behooves me to remind you that you are two and twenty and headed for the same fate, dearest. And I owe it to my beloved sister to help you make a prudent match."

"I will not leave Papa, not in his condition." Lora vehemently shook her head. "And I cannot leave *you*."

"Perdition! You cannot put my needs over yours. Oh no! That does not suit. Not when this house is more than either of us can manage."

"Never mind that." *You do not know the extent of my cousin's shortcomings.* More's the pity. If she did, Meg would sing a different tune. *Only one of us needs to carry that burden.* "We are managing very well."

"But for how long?"

"As long as it takes," she said, gazing out the window once more. The drizzling rain mirrored the melancholy constricting her heart. She dared not think about the future. It was a nauseating affair devoid of Nicholas. She neither wanted to marry nor needed a husband, especially not until she caught the person responsible for her brother's death. Papa was alive and thriving, though still slightly unstable on his feet. There was no need to worry about her safety, yet. Indeed, she was perfectly capable of taking care of herself. If her aunt found out what she did in the dark of night— "Papa will be back on his feet in due course. And perhaps this party will be exactly what he needs to make it so."

"I do hope you are right, Lora. Oh," Meg added energetically. "Did I mention your uncle was here earlier?"

"Uncle Thomas?" Her heart sank and a sudden queasiness took hold as tension built inside her. "You did not."

"We have received word that he is finally coming home."

"Who?" Though she knew the answer as a letter had arrived stating that her cousin Samuel had cashed in his commission at war's end.

"The Duke of Beresford."

Lora gazed at her aunt in shock. "The Duke of Beresford?"

This, indeed, was not the revelation she expected. She perched on the edge of the window seat, unexpectedly euphoric. *He has returned.* Myles Rutland, the Duke of Beresford, had been back to Kingston only once in two years—for his father's funeral—claiming London as his primary residence. The city she could not access due to her father's convalescence.

Predictably, he was the most sought-after bachelor in Town.

"I see something finally piqued your interest." Meg's endearing smile offset a teasing brow. "I am told he is keen to explore Kingston, and am happy to say that he will be joining our little house party." After a slight pause, she added, "As will Hawkesbury's son."

Lora's heart sank into her belly like an iron bucket plummeting down an empty well. "Thank you for apprising me of this news."

"'Tis not a plea for you to take precautionary measures. I beg you, give the man a chance to prove himself. War has changed men."

"Of course." Bile rose in her throat. *A leopard cannot change its spots.* "I shall try."

She did not trust Samuel. He was not an easy man to avoid, either. His whole life long, jealousy had fueled his spirit. If he desired something, he did not care who got in his way, frequently flying into fits of rage like a petulant child. Tormenting servants. Why, he'd even thrown tenants off the property without allowing the poor dears time to retrieve their belongings.

Another abhorrent offense—this one more reprehensible than the rest—was his claim that she was a pitiful wallflower in need of rescue. Cruel, despicable man! Was it any wonder? Until she'd attended her first Season in London, he'd purposefully scared off would-be suitors, intimidating anyone who threatened his governance. His efforts were for naught, however. Shadows did not scare her. Thanks to Papa's rare, unequalled devotion, and her exposure to reading, she understood what it was to be alive and thrive. The danger was not limited to the outdoors. Rather, deceit and disgrace were traps spun by people motivated by greed and ambition throughout all walks of life.

"I do hope the roads will be adequate for our guests." Meg searched the sky, the gloomy grey hanging over them, reflecting Lora's mood. "A few days of sun should do the trick."

If only it would be that easy to get rid of an unruly cousin.

Had Samuel returned from war a different man? She hoped so, for his father's sake. Uncle Thomas was a dignified man who deserved better. According to the servants, he suffered the worse for his only child's behavior but still kept the wolves at bay when Samuel's debts mounted, practically impoverishing him. That wayward solicitor's packet had revealed as much, and so, she'd left the evidence for her uncle to find.

Sympathy for Uncle Thomas's plight did not alter reality, however. She wanted nothing to do with his despicable son. And with Samuel present, what man in his right mind would dare approach her?

Not that she was looking for a husband. Conducting nightly raids in a bedchamber appealed more to a man. Not a woman determined to avenge her brother and be declared a public enemy. If discovered, her antics would cause ruin and humiliation.

Sulla said it best. *'No friend ever served me, and no enemy ever wronged me, whom I have not repaid in full.'*

Methods of trickery fueled revenge, making Lora a contradiction. She plotted and schemed, justifying her actions and interpreting the violent present. No one else would suffer the way her family had. And like Sulla, renaming himself Felix after his victory at Mithridates, she'd taken on the persona of a lady of vengeance, determined to rid this world of her foe's treachery.

But what did it matter where Samuel was concerned? He did not cherish family, and was incapable of loving anyone or anything. He wanted Winterbourne, Papa's title, wealth, and prestige. *Codswallop!* The country estate dated back hundreds of years, flourishing in plenty and privation. Papa had gone to great expense restoring it, pruning the wood, stocking the lake, overseeing the wildlife—the endeavor nearly costing him his life.

Marry her cousin? *How repugnant!* Whatever Samuel's alteration, in her mind, he still reeked of dung and deceit and despair after harassing Papa when she'd staunchly refused his hand. A drunken rage had followed, forcing Uncle Thomas to step in quickly and purchase his son a commission.

Only a tetched woman married the blackguard who connived against his own flesh and blood. If Samuel thought nothing of mistreating her father—and his own—what would he do to a disobedient wife?

She didn't intend to find out. She refused to submit to any man. Especially if her suspicions rang true and the person responsible for the hunting accident that injured her father was connected to her brother's murder. She'd hang a thousand lifetimes from a gibbet on the London Road like Jerry Abershawe for everyone to see in order to avenge Nicholas's death. And if her plans bore fruit, she would. Nothing could make her forget an assassin had killed her brother, the executioner feasting on her anguish as she helplessly watched.

Only one thing stood in her way—Lieutenant Samuel Hawkesbury.

She may not be the only outlaw in Surrey, but she would not get caught. Not when she was markedly close to discovering who pilfered and pillaged the inhabitants of Kingston when highwaymen were a thing of the past. The Duke of Beresford's absence, and his role as magistrate, had required that something be done, and quickly. His return, however, would put a damper on her well-laid plans.

"You are woolgathering again, Lora."

On the contrary. I am calculated, indomitable, and intent on saving us from unbearable servitude to the man who might one day call himself lord of—

"Assure me that you will be on your best behavior with our guests."

Soberly, she lowered her legs to the floor. Guests? Another reason why she objected to this party. Witnesses increased the risk of discovery. "I never put a foot wrong, Aunt."

"That is not what worries me. What worries me is whether that foot is silk-slippered and belongs to a lady."

She glanced down at her kid-leather half boots.

"Contrary to what you might think, I am a lady." Rain drenched the hillside, obscuring her vista of the rotunda, a reflection of the storm raging inside her. "You have nothing to fear. I would never tarnish our good name."

"That said, I require your promise."

"As you wish."

Meg squinted as she re-threaded her needle. "Lora."

"Very well. I promise." She rose from her perch, determination fueling her limbs. *Perhaps I have it all wrong. What if vengeance has hardened my heart beyond repair, irrevocably damning my soul, and there is no love left in me? What if there is no coming back from a life of hostility?*

She shook her head, resolved to find peace for Nicholas's soul, finality. Conceivably, it would be easier to move on. But a nefarious game was afoot, and she intended to keep her enemies close. If only she could find out who her enemies were. More than one roved the countryside, causing mayhem. She'd wounded a man robbing the widow Marlowe's house at the same time the townspeople said a thief had stolen twenty pounds from The Hog's Head.

A troublesome dilemma, especially since she had yet to find the man with the orange neckerchief.

She wasn't daft. It is unlikely that Samuel, who hadn't been seen for a year, could have been involved by proxy. At least she wouldn't discount the possibility. And if that was the case, his attendance at Winterbourne allowed opportunities for discovery. However, the only impediment to that plan required her to put herself in the line of sight.

She shivered at the repulsive thought. Half the battle to getting Samuel to admit his crimes was the proven experience that he could be baited.

Bait him, she would.

"I must go." She strode to Meg, kissing her cheek when her aunt gave her a withering look. "To confer with Cook. When our guests arrive, they will require dry linen and refreshment."

"Lora," Meg warned.

"Put your mind at ease. I will play my part." She flashed a broad smile. "You have my vow that I will manage everything with the utmost care."

"Why am I not convinced?"

"Am I not your favorite niece?"

A ripple of mirth escaped Meg. "You are my only niece."

"And you've proven my point." Flashing her aunt a warm smile, she giggled, then strolled into the long hall, the thrill of the hunt seizing her spirit as a flurry of servants just as ambitious as she scurried past.

Winterbourne had once been a thriving estate, filled with music, joy, and laughter, the purity allowing for explorations of the heart stripped away after her father's ill-timed injury. Following a season of silent reflection and a deafening reduction of amusement, a charged current now swirled inside her like a stream of wasteful energy.

Though she'd participated in several seasons, she cared nothing for the social set. She preferred the country. There, Papa had showered her with attention, extending the same care he'd shown Nicholas, training them both in the arts of conservancy and gentlemanly sport. His horrific fall from a horse during a hunt and his subsequent lengthy recovery process had forced Nicholas to handle their affairs. Her brother, in turn, had consulted her in the presence of solicitors, insisting they handle every facet of their existence at Winterbourne together, while honing pursuits like reading and riding and nightly games of chess by the fire.

Now Nicholas was gone, and everything fell on her. If

she'd been born a man, no one would dare question the future of the estate or force her to marry.

I can protect myself.

Her aunt's invitation to lords and ladies and gentry, with the caveat that Lora must marry, was a slight against the serenity and solitude Lora sought.

Marry my own cousin? "Bah!"

The life of a female was more complex than marrying and producing an heir and a spare, though that had been the way of things for centuries. Every creature on Earth had a mother. *But not at the cost of my independence. The freedom to ride astride without complaint. To manage and explore the estate without interference. To play the pianoforte at any hour. To read until dawn or rise and lay down at my own convenience.*

In retrospect, these were extravagances the average woman could ill afford. Except, this was *Lora's life*, no one else's. And no man would take away her freedom without her consent, especially a wayfaring cousin who'd run off to war to avoid debt collectors.

Samuel was a gambler and a lout, if the receipts she'd seen from debt collectors were any indication. Nevertheless, when he arrived, Winterbourne would become *his* hunting grounds for nigh on a month and she wasn't quite sure how to handle that unsettling situation—yet. Discouraging her cousin would not solve issues of inheritance, for those were bound by law and precedence. The bigger challenge would require a ceasefire, a scheme she wasn't sure she could abide.

But how did one welcome home the man who intended to turn her world upside down?

She stopped in her tracks, a spasm of delight rushing through her veins.

If Papa were to remarry—

CHAPTER 3

*L*onely stretches of land spread out before Myles as he made his way to Kingston, attended at equal distances on the London Road by toll takers. He enjoyed being connected to the earth by hoof. It allowed for experiencing the countryside rather than spending hours insulated in a carriage. Preferring to ride alone, he'd sent his valet, Higgins, and private secretary, Clifford Henry, ahead in the conveyance to announce his impending arrival at his estate. While the journey used to be dangerous for riders and coaches alike, criminals like Jerry Abershawe were no longer a threat as tolls made it harder for highwaymen to escape, which also increased the flow of traffic and the ease of travel.

Passing Abershawe's old haunts, Wimbledon Common and then the Bald-Faced Stag on the edge of Richmond Park, a deer darted out across the road. The sighting made Myles ponder how long it would take for London's infringing perimeters to completely overrun nature in all its simplicity. Expansion allowed for convenience, but it also encouraged illegal activity. Like the actions perfected by the highway-woman Grimes had described.

Nearly home now, he wondered what type of woman broke the law without fear of the consequences.

Paltry crimes—though the harm done to Grimes's person could hardly be called trifling—eventually led to more desperate and gruesome acts. Like the murder of the marquess's son, the Earl of Norbiton.

Was there a connection? Records stated the pike of a crossbow shot had felled the young earl from a wooded area, the earl becoming vulnerable to the fatal blow as he rode in the open.

In the twilight, a shrill cry pierced the night, followed by frantic, shouting voices, each one echoing through the wood and originating from the grounds of his estate, held in the Rutlands' possession for the past two hundred years.

Startled, he kicked his heels, spurring his horse on, cursing the winding, wooded road that prevented him easier access to the house. The long drive leading there offered visitors a grand view of the property, as well as the lake, rotunda, and flora and fauna. Hardly beneficial to a man hellbent on arriving in a hurry.

A soft mist drifted over the road, distorting the route. Moisture hung in the air, infiltrating his lungs. Alarm surged through his veins, boiling his blood as he urged his mount faster.

Encroaching darkness cast shadows, tree limbs swinging low and posing dangerous obstacles to his advance. Sundown was upon them, the moon rising to illuminate the fog and provide just enough light to keep his horse from stepping into a hole.

Gun shots!

He thinned his lips, cursing his delay. Perhaps things were worse than he had originally imagined. Maybe Grimes's accusations had put the wrong ideas in his head. Or was the area completely overrun by bandits? And were those blackguards even now disrupting those under the Rutlands' care at Darby House?

Speeding around the lake, chaos unfolded before him. Servants were setting off on foot for the woods, armed and giving chase, while his private secretary stormed down the steps rising to the main residence, ordering servants about and dispersing them in numerous directions.

Myles's mind reeled, his heart seizing. Something was wrong, terribly wrong, and he hadn't been there to stop it. He hadn't been there—again.

"Yer Grace!" Potts, his stablemaster, bellowed. "Ye are a sight for these sore eyes. It does me 'eart good to see that ye arrived safely. But I fear ye are too late."

Too late? What did that mean? He quickly reined in his horse, gravel skidding as his mount came to a halt. "What's the matter? What's happened?"

"Two men broke into the main 'ouse."

Two men? That ruled out Grimes's highwaywoman. That someone dared to break into Darby, a ducal residence, filled him with unmitigated rage. "How long ago?"

"Yer Grace—"

"How long?" he shouted, circling his horse and desiring to give chase.

Potts grabbed the reins. "Stuart discovered them." His strained expression filled Myles with apprehension. "They got away."

No need to worry then. Stuart, his butler, must have repelled them. He scanned the woods, consumed by impatience. "How long ago?" he repeated.

"Thirty minutes. Maybe more, Yer Grace."

What had the thieves been looking for? He planned to confer with Stuart once he settled everything. "Scour the woods. Summon everyone—tenants, croft owners. Remind them to be on their guard. Outlaws are dangerous."

"Already done, Yer Grace."

He glanced around, finding it odd that Stuart wasn't present. "Where's Stuart?"

"He's—"

"This way!" came a yell in the semi-darkness. Both Myles and Potts instantly shot a look to the wood line where several men appeared, waving them on. "This way!"

Instinct took over. Without another thought, he kicked his heels and arrowed his mount in that direction.

"But Yer Grace. There's somethin' ye must know. Stuart—"

Potts's shout quickly faded as Myles raced on, determined to catch the intruders. When he reached the edge of the wood, the men shouted and pointed east, saying they had seen a rider in the timberland. He leaned forward in the saddle, elbows bent, understanding the risk both to himself and his mount as he hurdled a log and rode into the woods, offering thanks that his groundskeepers kept the trees neatly trimmed for the hunt; low branches blinded men and beast alike.

Mist coated the forest floor, preventing him from tracking the thieves, the damp smell eerily following him as he worked his way through the trees and scanned for signs of his prey. Moonlight shone through layers of latticed leaves, and the wind whistled and pulsated above the great canopy, cascading down like a wave. Young and old boughs creaked. The soft, stuttering rhythm of an owl met his ears. A fox yipped in the distance.

Then he heard it—a horse wuffling. Two or three short inhales followed by a forceful exhale indicated his target was a short distance ahead. A soft whinny and a nervous stamp. Both signaled his quarry moved without haste, almost as if hunting something else.

The novelty of giving chase immediately wore off and

alarm intensified inside him, a hostile reminder that he'd ridden straight into the lion's den without a plan.

The faint sound of men calling to one another infiltrated the trees. He rode on deeper and deeper into the wood, moonlight and mist helping and hindering his advance. Bypassing a low branch, he chanced to look northward and caught a flash of red and white.

He blinked.

I'll be damned.

A white horse, and seated upon it, a red-cloaked rider.

Could this be Grimes's highwaywoman?

Lost in his thoughts, he misjudged his course, and his mount stepped on a branch, the sound loud enough to make the mysterious figure stop dead in her tracks. The entire experience gave him seconds to process the sight before him.

The head beneath the draped hood snapped to attention, his position spotted in an instant. Indecision and desperation radiated off the figure in waves. Then, without warning, she coaxed her horse forward and off into the wood they sped.

His heartbeat quickened as he directed his mount into motion, eyes on his quarry and attempting to outflank her. But his adversary proved swifter, lighter, knowledgeable of the terrain and more capable of navigating the woods. City life, it appeared, had made him soft. And before he had the chance to solve the identity of the red-cloaked highway-woman, she disappeared almost as fast as she'd materialized out of the mist.

Slowing his horse to a halt, he struggled to fathom what he'd just experienced. *Grimes's highwaywoman is flesh and blood, no tall tale to assuage a man's pride!*

The red hooded cloak. The white horse. He had a conundrum to solve.

He was chewing over this information when a shout interrupted his thoughts. "Yer Grace!"

Turning, he spotted several men advancing toward him. He reined his mount to face them. "Did you see her?"

"Who?" one man he remembered from his youth named Hyde said.

"The highwaywoman."

"No, Yer Grace. We were chasin' the two men who got away."

The two men who got away? "The woman clad in red isn't the one you were after?"

Hyde shrugged. "Two troublemakers plyin' their trade in the country broke into the house, Yer Grace."

"Best be gettin' back now, Hyde," a tenant named Sanders said. "They'll be no sleepin' tonight, Yer Grace. Not after—"

"What?" he asked. "What else has happened?"

Hyde's eyes widened in alarm until Myles thought they would pop out of the man's skull. "Ye do not know?"

Sanders and Hyde exchanged strange expressions, rendering Myles speechless. What were they hiding? He shot a withering glance over his shoulder and squinted at the chaos still occurring up at the house. Resigned to discover what was going on, he jerked the reins and dashed out of the woods.

Nothing made sense. "I'll find out myself."

The murder of a young earl. A highwaywoman, her red-clad figure hunting, like him, on his grounds for what he knew not. Thievery. The affront of someone breaking into a ducal residence.

These were not coincidences.

When a man stole into another man's home, it was a deliberate act. But for what purpose? The Rutlands' philanthropic work extended hundreds of miles, to include almost every district in the kingdom. The house contained elegant furniture, silver and china, of course. It had once been a hubbub of entertainment, hosting parties and festivals for the locals. But, without a duchess, the family jewels were no longer kept on the premises.

Who dared to break into Darby?

Dismounting near the entrance to his familial home, anger surged within him. He strode up the stairs, then stopped cold on the threshold. Women filled the atrium, surrounding his housekeeper and several moaning maids who bent over someone on the parquet floor.

Hell, and the Devil! Had the intruders injured one of his own?

This was not to be borne!

"What is going on?" he demanded, pushing his way through the sobbing women.

What met his eyes pilfered his breath.

Stuart.

The reason his butler had not been at his post became clear. He could not man it. *Damn me, I should have known!* Blood spilled from Stuart's faultless attire onto the pristine marble floor.

"Stuart?" Rushing to his side, Myles's heart seized, squeezing his chest cruelly. "Dear God, man, what has happened? Who did this to you?"

"They—" Stuart attempted to rise, but collapsed, wincing. "Two."

"Two?"

"Henchmen."

"Remain still, sir," he advised, not wanting Stuart to exasperate his injury or cause himself further pain. Though women attempted to assist Stuart, he shot a them a frustrated look, feeling utterly helpless. Needing a miracle. "Do something. Stop the bleeding!"

"We've tried, Your Grace. He is . . . He is—"

"No time." Stuart wheezed.

"He refused to let them pass," Mrs. Warren volunteered,

shaking her head to warn Myles that Stuart's injuries were fatal.

Indeed, a closer look at the dark color of blood signified severe internal damage. Myles bowed his head, incapable of believing the proof before his eyes. He grabbed Stuart's hand, barely able to hold back his misery or the catch in his voice. "Why did you confront them?"

Stuart smiled wanly, the effort costing him dearly. Old and frail, the butler had dutifully served the family long before Myles's birth. The stoic man's exceptional style, unquestionable loyalty, and bright, unchecked wit had been a buoy in times of trouble and a comfort in times of plenty.

"Your life is worth more than anything this house offers."

"My . . ." A deathly pallor overtook Stuart. "Duty—"

"Duty be damned, man! Think no more about the estate. Conserve your energy. You must recover." He choked back his anguish. "You must. I need you."

"Not." Stuart perked briefly. "Anymore."

What did he mean? Not anymore? "You are essential to life here. To me. You must fight. FIGHT, Stuart!"

"Fare . . . well." Pain wracked the butler's body. He reached up weakly to touch Myles's cheek. "My . . . boy."

With a cringing, frightening gasp, Stuart inhaled his last breath. The gruesome sound vibrated through Myles's bones. A lump rose in his throat but he quickly banished the tears that threatened to come, commanding himself to be strong in front of his household staff.

Mrs. Warren shrieked.

The maids groaned with loud, heart-wrenching sobs.

Stuart.

A low growl erupted from Myles as he gently lowered the man's hand and closed his unseeing eyes. Images flashed before him. A childhood filled with laughter and lessons. Stuart silencing him when he spoke out of turn. The occasional nudge given when he refused to put the right foot forward. The unequaled insistence that honor and duty prevailed over everything else. The quiet reassurances that had steered Myles through the worst events of his life—the death of his father, his rise to a dukedom and the responsibilities he shouldered to the tenants and croft owners in the vale. He'd cherished Stuart's wisdom and leadership, and yes, his friendship, knowing they didn't have a typical master-servant relationship. Yet, the whole was a marvel. The respect he had for Stuart's sense of duty and the care with which he kept Darby and those under his supervision in line without selfish reservation had meant everything to them all.

In hindsight, Stuart's lifelong devotion was the last link to his father. And now, he was gone. *Taken. Stolen.* And nothing would stop him from locating and punishing whoever was responsible. Nothing!

Summoning control, Myles knew that, first and foremost, he had to get to the root of what happened. Stuart had not said thieves or robbers had entered the house and killed him. He'd used the word 'henchmen.' The dutiful butler had never spoken without clear intent before, so that must be a clue. Henchmen danced to the demands of puppet masters, people powerful enough to sway men into thievery and murder.

But Stuart had stopped them, thwarting their objective. The question now begged: What could they have been searching for? Whatever it was, they hadn't got it.

"Yer Grace."

The only way to locate the henchmen is to know thine enemy.

"Yer Grace."

Clenching his fists, he closed his eyes, willing the memory of Stuart lying in a pool of blood to fade. *Impossible.*

"The thieves 'ave escaped, Yer Grace."

His groundskeeper's voice cut through the thorny bramble, restricting his attention. "What?" he asked, turning to the man who was speaking.

"They're gone," Cobb said, his flushed face and dodging eyes revealing that he'd rather be elsewhere. "What would ye have us do?"

"Every minute is crucial." His staff depended on him to make the correct decisions through misery and despair.

But he was not the only one mourning Stuart's death. The maids wept and clung to one another. Mrs. Warren, God love her, knelt to rearrange Stuart's clothing carefully to restore his ghastly appearance.

"It is late and dark and there is little else to do for Stuart now. Go," he said. "See that everyone returns home. We shall meet early in the morning to discuss what needs to be done."

"What about Stuart, Yer Grace?" Cobb asked.

"Carry him into the red parlor."

"Beggin' yer pardon, Yer Grace, but wouldn't it be better to—"

"No." He whipped around on Cobb, unable to contain his anger.

He'd lost so much. And now, someone dear to the estate, to the household, to him, had been erased.

Cobb and several others shuffled in to lift Stuart's body.

Biting back the weighty turmoil roiling through his blood, he added, "After you place Stuart in the red parlor, Mrs. Warren and I shall take care of him." Indeed, he planned to study Stuart's body for evidence that might lead to his killer. After that, everyone else could pay their respects. "Go now," he said, dismissing the lot when their work was done. "Leave me."

When the last had crossed the threshold and closed the door quietly behind them, he stared down at Darby's loyal champion. The old guard had aged more than he realized, lines etched into the skin around his eyes and mouth, his wrinkled forehead a map of censured thoughts. What had they been, and why had he waited until it was too late to wonder what Stuart would have told him if he'd been free to impart wisdom?

The butler had been a symbol of all that was well and good at Darby. And the gut-wrenching truth was that Myles wasn't sure if Darby would ever recover from Stuart's absence.

While the land and the house symbolized permanence, containing sculptures, paintings, an extensive library, luxurious rooms and halls, fountains, a lake and a folly, Rutlands hadn't built the estate to repel intruders. It had no hidden passageways, turrets, and towers for defense. There'd never been a need.

The attempted robbery and Stuart's death changed that.

Logic returned. This was no isolated incident. Someone knowledgeable in Darby's location had orchestrated it. But who? Who would dare send henchmen to Darby and for what purpose?

He placed Stuart's hands across his chest, blood staining his fingers. "I will find whoever did this and bring them to justice."

But where would his search lead? And was the highway-woman a pivotal piece of the puzzle?

CHAPTER 4

The day of Winterbourne's ball, a steady sea of fashionable city and country folk arrived to test propriety and passion, and forge bonds in a landscape of embellishments; wax candles in cut-glass chandeliers, lusters, and lamps illuminated rooms thrown open for the occasion. Plants from the conservatory and hot-house flowers transformed the interior of the house, teasing the senses, while politicians hobnobbed with their betters. Gossips remarked on the number of couples, the make of gowns, manners and good looks. All while music and dancing heightened expectations that the next three weeks would be a memorable experience leading into autumn.

A welcome breeze wafted from the open veranda doors, providing Lora relief from the overcrowded space. The refinement and refreshments, mockery, and merriment created a magical realm that contrasted reality, a fact she found frustrating. People brought chaos and demands. They required attention, preventing her from acting on impulse.

Pretending to be a wallflower—a pair of spectacles and a mousy demeanor her only armor—she played her part lest she disappoint Aunt Meg. Balls were feasts of artifice and flirtation, tombs of intrigue and interrogation that led women to ruin. She abhorred frippery, folly, and the foppish behavior allowed in ballrooms, preferring the splendor of nature, the outdoors, and the crisp country air to the rich and classical bouquet of beeswax and boredom. In truth, Society did not recommend her, though that had not always been the case.

Nicholas's horrific death had changed everything. Nothing would ever be the same.

Aunt Meg and Uncle Thomas led off the first set, *Lady Montgomery*, while everyone danced simultaneously in one singular line over the tastefully chalked floor, decorated with symbolic scenes of victory. It had been Meg's idea to honor Kingston's veterans of militia regiments and volunteers, who were flocking home in droves. Other dances followed with *Juliana*, a Viennese waltz, enlivening the room, providing a rare chance for the unwed to exude power and persuasion over the opposite sex. Now people who'd scarcely shaken hands had permission to affect a tender touch like an affianced lover under the watchful eyes of doting mamas.

"Isn't the waltz thrilling?" her friend Lady Elizabeth Seymore asked with a flood of enthusiasm meant to inspire Lora into a sigh. "Oh, look, there's Lady Anne. Take note of her hem as she spins. The drape and swirl of her gown adds an ethereal beauty to the dance, does it not?" Indeed, Lady Anne and those around her came to life, twirling, swaying, and gliding as gracefully as swans on a lake. "Oh, to be swept about in such a manner, dizzy with delight and dreaming about a lover's touch throughout the night."

"Eliza," Lora whispered, noticing the matrons around them blushing as their younger daughters traversed the floor in the arms of strangers, "someone will overhear."

"Let them hear. It is not as if anyone pays attention to me anyway."

"They should. You deserve better." A violent seizure of Lora's affections took hold. Although she and Eliza were childhood friends, women like them—wallflowers—sat and waited, left to rot between potted palms and partitions, their hopes of dancing face-to-face with a heroic gentleman dashed to smithereens. Reserve was not at fault for the ratio of male to female guests. Dowries and a lack of flirtation cursed those without. "I suppose dancing with an amiable partner poses an entertaining diversion, but dreaming about such a one depends on the man, his constitution, his morals, his—"

"Any man will do."

"Eliza, you shouldn't say such things." Her scandalous remark filled Lora with dread. Desperation had ruined innocents, and that was not a fate she desired Eliza to endure. "Be careful what you wish for."

"Don't be such a bird-wit. I am not wicked. You know what I mean." Eliza covered her mouth, stifling a giggle. "Oh, but I fly ahead of myself again. Of course, I would have to be asked to dance. Instead, I wait to be claimed by a *worthy* gentleman, which would be a Herculean feat, providing I was not—"

"A wallflower?" Pesky mark, that. "You are not. In any sense of the word. I beg, do not contemplate the idea. Why, you just danced with Mr. Grimes." She pressed her lips together to keep from grinning as the solicitor's subtle limp guaranteed he'd gotten the point. When she'd blocked Mr. Grimes's access to her uncle's property, she'd had no intention of permanently harming the man. Far from it. His blatant refusal to allow her access to his dispatches, however, followed by his cowardly actions, had got him into trouble.

Visits to her uncle had become more frequent, and with

news that Samuel would return, curiosity made her wonder if the increased activity had anything to do with her cousin selling his commission. The time for glossing over Samuel's gambling habits was at an end. And based on what she'd learned, should Samuel inherit Winterbourne, he would drive the whole of it to destitution in a matter of weeks, using the estate as collateral.

"Poor old man," Eliza went on, though forty could hardly be called old. Meg was forty-two. "The effort caused him immeasurable pain."

What had the solicitor told her? She suddenly grew uncomfortable. "How so?"

"Did you not hear? He was attacked by highwaymen a fortnight ago."

"Highwaymen?" The man's ridiculous admission was not shocking. What was surprising was a sudden desire to tell Eliza the truth. If she knew the lengths to which Lora had gone to avenge Nicholas, what would her friend think of her? "The tolls have—"

"Yes. Yes, I know. It is typically safer to travel along that route now." Eliza shot her a look, her green eyes gleaming like porcelain as they locked onto Lora's. "I believe him. While valiantly protecting a woman in his care, he stated he was outflanked and shot."

Lora gasped. Not because the wound intensified her guilt, but for the inflated lies which would now become legend.

"Oh, it is a gut-wrenching tale, I assure you. The poor lady in his care swooned."

What a barrow of bollocks! Grimes's drivers had abandoned him and he had no spine.

"Mr. Grimes confronted the highwaymen, using his sword to repel them, but he was struck down from behind. Thankfully, due to his heroic actions, the damsel he rescued was there to provide him with sufficient care. And lo, he is here to tell the tale."

A warning voice whispered not to engage. Mr. Grimes's cowardice and bloated fable revealed him to be a warty frog. "Your beauty is mesmerizing, and dancing with Mr. Grimes allowed him to overcome his affliction. Take heart." Other gentlemen surely noticed her beauty and poise as she danced with a disagreeable partner. "Others will flock to your side. Wait and see."

Gathering her dearest friend close, quashing fears that Eliza may go home disappointed—yet again—she could not hold back the rush of reassurances that spilled from her mouth. They provided no solace when she was in a similar situation—a product of her own making, no less. She had no plans to show the strength of her power. She was a secondary object, the daughter of the host, nothing more. She intended to fade into the woodwork. For it was there she could plot and plan, determining the muster of men, condemning or exonerating them at her leisure.

"You are the prettiest creature present, Eliza." Which wasn't a lie. Eliza's dowry, however, limited temptation. "One of these *fine* gentlemen will come to his senses and fall prostrate at your feet, blathering on about the color of your hair or your winsome, tempting eyes. Perhaps I should retrieve the smelling salts."

That bit of wit produced a chuckle.

"Seriously, believe me when I say it is only a matter of time before someone sweeps you off your feet."

"The Duke of Beresford."

At that announcement, Eliza grabbed her arm abruptly. "He has come. I thought the rumors must be false. Oh, my heart is aflutter. Do you think it possible he might ask us to dance?"

"I can hardly say," Lora said unable to pull her gaze away

from the handsome figure the duke posed standing there, dressed in black from head to foot, a white stock hugging his rugged jaw and a perfectly tied cravat the only adornment.

"It would be the height of rudeness to refuse him."

Yes. It was universally acknowledged that if a woman turned down a man, she must turn down all the others. A challenge Lora did not welcome, especially when Papa and Meg had such high hopes of her marrying by Season's end. No one would do for her except the duke. His handsome face frequented her dreams, and the memory of the look in his soul-stirring eyes as he'd chased her in the woods made her fear that he blamed her for his butler's death. Nothing could be further from the truth. She'd had no part in the poor man's demise and could also not afford the distraction the duke posed for her. She was determined to bring Nicholas's killer to justice. And if that meant sacrificing any future she might have had with the duke, so be it.

Eliza shook her out of her musings. "According to Wightman, we must *'respect, cultivate, and exalt'* the strength of our power. It is said to link us to angels."

Lora smiled, then looked away from the duke, fearful he'd catch her staring. "I am not an angel."

"Whatever do you mean, Lora? You are the most angelic person I know."

Which beggared belief. If her dearest friend knew her, really knew her—what she'd done to Mr. Grimes, the depths to which she'd fallen to catch a killer—she'd emerge from the shadows of their lifelong friendship and never look back.

After his name was announced, Myles entered the Marquess of Putney's ballroom and patiently waited for the games to begin. No matter the invitation, the marriage mart was an inevitable albatross hanging over every eligible gentleman's head—especially his.

To emphasize his point, the heads of peers of the realm, gentry and wealthy merchants immediately snapped to attention at the announcement of his presence, eyes rounding on him like hawks espying prey, hovering vertically, and slowly rattling teeth. Was it any wonder why he avoided the preposterous pomp, the hypocrisy, and the strict rules that held him aloft even in the country? Men weren't born great, but forged in fire and tried, earning respect from a lifetime of service to the Crown. Responsibility outweighed selfish inclinations, though there were those who sneered at their due and destroyed the living as quickly as swatting an insect from the air.

Returning the astonished stares of those who studied him, he said to no one in particular, "So, it begins."

Winterbourne.

The place where dreams ended. The home of the only young lady who'd ever tempted him, and the one he'd avoided at all cost—Lady Lora Putney. There were hints that the extravagances and details provided this country house party were plotted and planned, for all intents and purposes, to secure Lora a suitable husband. But which had captured her heart? A nobleman? A country squire, local vicar, farmer? And why did the idea of her marrying another bother him? He had no claim on the marquess's daughter. Why, he didn't know her and, like a damn fool, had never allowed himself the opportunity to do so.

The musicians returned to their work while Grimes's accusations, the attempted robbery at Darby, and Stuart's murder, tugged at him, shifting his perspective back to important matters. There was no help to be had for this current commitment. Even at the cost of avoiding a diamond of the first water.

Bollocks! This misery was damned inconvenient, nauseating even, leaving him to wade into murky depths. One step into Winterbourne forced him to acknowledge that he could no longer ignore the facts. Against his machinations and the powers of persuasion, a wallflower owned him body and soul. *Him.* A duke! And the unforeseeable hiccup of their troubled past gutted cruelly, like a bayonet fixed on an attacking foe.

Except he was staring back at his own face.

Best come to terms with the decisions he'd made, a blunder of epic proportions meant to protect his heart. The damage had been done. To her. To him. The moon would fall from the sky before Lora would ever forgive his coldness, or he Fate, for the vastly different roads their paths had taken.

Too late, he'd come to the realization that he couldn't purge Lora from his soul. And now, there was no way to make amends. Her father's serious injury in a hunting accident kept her from participating in the marriage market. Then his father had died of natural causes, jettisoning his life into mourning as he assumed his new role. And woe betide them, Fate had struck again when someone murdered her brother, cutting him down squarely in his youth.

He'd made inquiries, unearthed no answers, and felt equally unqualified to offer the grieving solace. What man had the power to alter the past for himself or another? If he had, restoring a most beloved brother, indeed, the young Earl of Norbiton, to life would have been his first work. But only God had that kind of governance over mankind. So, life had gone on as it always had, in dreary fashion, season after season revolving with no resolution in sight.

How was he to know whether a young lady desired to marry the man he'd become or a dukedom? Fate didn't deal fairly. The events close to home of late were a prime example of that incontestable fact.

Nevertheless, here he was, having never attended a ball in Kingston-upon-Thames as the Duke of Beresford. Eton and Oxford, and timetables and tasks, had occupied him elsewhere as the Season and Society demanded. But current events—the haunts of highwaymen and Stuart's gruesome death—overruled despondency, disaster, and distance.

He'd best remember why he'd come to Winterbourne. Not for pleasure. And most certainly not for Lady Lora before she duly wed.

As magistrate, people expected him to wade through muck and uncover clues to the red-clad thief who was last seen leaving his property. And the only way to gradually gain favor with the locals was to reveal the identity of that despicable woman in the midst of it all. Although few people with good sense discussed peculiar matters with virtual strangers.

He focused on the sea of bobbing heads. Good manners and genuflections, flirtations and fancy were in plentiful supply as the musicians restarted *Juliana*, the mellifluous strains revitalizing the atmosphere.

Before too long, hesitancy to approach him waned, and a welcoming officiant advanced with a proper bow. "You honor us with your presence, Your Grace. Allow me to provide you with a warm Winterbourne welcome."

"And you are?" he asked, aware, too late, that he sounded

pompous.

"Philip Stanhope, at your service, Your Grace."

He clasped his hands behind his back. "Ah. The marquess's solicitor."

"Indeed. I am honored that you know who I am, Your Grace."

"I make it a habit to learn everything about the people I have to thank for grand invitations."

Tall and lithe, Stanhope's genuine smile made the man instantly likable. "If I may be so bold, we were uncertain you would attend. It is the first time you've accepted an invitation from Kingston-upon-Thames."

"Yes," he said, bitten by regret. "Time has not been my own."

Another bow, this one more clipped. "My condolences, Your Grace, of course. May I offer you a private room in Winterbourne? It is His Lordship's hope that you will make use of it for the remainder of the party."

Though proximity to Lady Lora might be insufferably hard to bear, the situation provided him more time to investigate the happenings in Kingston. He tilted his head in thanks. "Delightful."

"If you will allow me to say so, Your Grace, your father was a good man."

He offered a quick nod as he searched the room. It did not differ from the more sophisticated establishments in London, filled as it was with matchmaking mamas, gesticulating fans and encouraging their daughters to pose to full effect. *A hornet's nest.* "Yes, I do say he was." He paused. "Stanhope, would you do me the honor of introductions? I have been preoccupied for far too long and I have not had the pleasure of meeting my neighbors."

An expression of wonder transformed Stanhope's face. "It would be an honor, Your Grace."

The man stepped back, gesturing for Myles to accompany him. Guests offered them a wide berth as they passed. Wives, daughters and sons, and several uniformed men bowed and curtsied reverently. All because he was a duke. Not for who he was or what he stood for, but for a hereditary title.

"If I may, Your Grace." Stanhope gestured to a group of men gathered by the hearth. "There, you will find the Honorable Thomas Hawkesbury and his son."

"Hawkesbury." Grimes's client, in the flesh. "The marquess's brother, if I am not mistaken."

"Yes, Your Grace." The man's demeanor swiftly changed. "After the death of the marquess's son, he stands to inherit should—"

"Understood," he said as several couples walked past, arm-in-arm.

The pause enabled Myles to see that Stanhope was devoted to his master, Putney, and he strongly objected to the idea of losing the marquess. "From your tone, I take it you disapprove."

"Of his brother? Heavens, no. Although, if anything happens to Hawkesbury—"

"You may speak freely," he said, desiring to learn as much as he could about the dynamics of the village. "The truth is all I seek."

"I confess, Your Grace, my personal opinions are my own. I am a simple solicitor in the marquess' service and do not wish to influence—"

"But your profession endorses honesty, does it not?" He took in the merriment, recalling his youth and the occasions when Kingston had celebrated the harvest. "I insist."

"Very well." Stanhope nodded stiffly. "In the event something happens to Hawkesbury, the title will pass to the man's son. In that, I regret I have no say." He turned to reveal more with caution. "And it troubles me to admit the marquess's brother hasn't been himself of late. My concern for Lord Putney and his brother grows by the day."

"May I ask why?"

Stanhope nodded to someone he knew. "Forgive me for saying so, but I have it on good authority that young Hawkesbury is a rakehell. And if that is still the case, his return to Kingston is not in anyone's best interest, especially mine."

Myles studied the fellow with the acute ability to weed out the chaff. "Go on."

"He's been known to drink heavily, gamble excessively, offend the ladies, and the list goes on. Decorum dictates, however, that the marquess extends his family every courtesy."

"Of course." Myles examined young Hawkesbury, who stood in his regimentals, his chest expanding with overblown satisfaction. In his dealings with the Admiralty, he'd witnessed a man or two altered by wartime commissions. Was Hawkesbury such a man? "War changes men."

"Some for the better," Stanhope replied grimly. "Some not."

"And the marquess? Is he in attendance?"

"Regrettably, no. His daughter is present. She is there, modestly dressed and standing with the other young ladies assembled by the refreshment table."

He searched the bevy of young swans glancing in his direction. Pearls and ribbons adorned each fancy head, and jewels glistened around graceful necks. Hopeful expressions lit faces with curiosity and delight, but he did not plan to be swayed by fancy and flirtation. He hadn't come to form attachments. He wasn't in the market for a wife. Not when his butler's murderer roamed the countryside, and a bewitching woman in a red cloak held the key to the answers he sought.

The musicians created an ethereal atmosphere, and the wedge protecting the marquess's daughter thinned as he watched one young pen after another flock elsewhere, abandoning the last three. Before them, surefooted dancers basked in the refinement and splendor equal to lavish aristocratic events he'd attended in the city.

"If you'll follow me, I'll make the introductions."

He dragged his eyes away from Lora. "Thank you."

Stanhope worked his way through the crush. If anyone knew what was going on in Kingston-upon-Thames, it would be the marquess. Despite the man's choice not to make an appearance, it is possible that he was resting in an anti-room or library nearby, and an audience could be obtained through his only living child.

Dancers laughed gaily, their merriment contrasting wildly with the fierce impulses flowing through him to kill the man responsible for Stuart's death—the contradiction catching him off guard. His height offered advantage as they progressed, providing him an intriguing panorama the further they moved into the room, faces and speech put to memory.

Whilst players attended whist tables positioned in an adjacent room, making bets they hoped to win, men wallowed in self-importance, ignoring the disappointed hopes of women seated along the walls. A place, he noticed, Lora no longer occupied.

Candelabras illuminated the whole, beeswax and heat a heady mix. Refreshments beckoned, all manner of delectable fruits, roasted pheasant and fowl, and a profusion of flowers presented on silver, crystal, and exquisite French china. The marquess had spared no expense. Nevertheless, nothing would be more satisfying than obtaining an audience with Putney.

What would he have to do to get one?

CHAPTER 5

*M*yles had a lot to atone for, and there were no guarantees that Lady Lora would receive him if she remembered that night at the Templeton's ball and his callous disregard for her feelings.

He followed Stanhope through the crowded room, his height providing a clear view of bobbing heads, and bodies orchestrating movements like a flock of hungry gulls diving and surfacing, wings expanding and retracting, wave after roiling wave across the floor until he found himself delivered to a pair of young women standing by a potted palm.

There, Stanhope cleared his throat. The two wallflowers turned, and in an instant, Myles came face-to-face with the one young woman he'd been running from for several years —the Marquess of Putney's daughter.

"Ladies," Stanhope said with a bow. "The Duke of Beresford has requested an introduction. Your Grace, allow me to present Lady Lora Putney and Lady Elizabeth Seymore."

He bowed stiffly as the two women dipped a curtsy.

Lora, in particular, made a show of pushing a pair of

spectacles onto the bridge of her nose and scrunching her nostrils.

Strange. The last time he'd seen her, she hadn't had poor eyesight.

"How do you do, Your Grace," the two young ladies said in unison.

Before he could respond, Stanhope presented his hand to Lady Elizabeth. "Lady Elizabeth, would you do me the honor of this dance?"

Lady Elizabeth flashed a radiant smile and a quick glance at Lora before accepting Stanhope's hand. "I would be delighted, sir."

"Excuse us," Stanhope said conveniently.

Myles watched the friendly solicitor escort Lady Elizabeth to the dance floor, then turned his attention to Lora.

The moment he'd both dreaded and dreamed of for three years had finally come.

Lora peered up at him, quirking a brow. "You honor us with your presence, Your Grace. My father will be terribly unhappy to have missed your arrival. It has always been his dearest hope you would attend."

"I am disappointed." He studied the picture Lora painted with her artfully arranged brown hair, and her eyes glittering behind glass like heated amber, the effect helping the minimal amount of frippery adorning her person to accentuate her beautiful face. Prim and proper, her stiff posture and stare were unyielding. She didn't appear impressed by his title, the ball, the music, or lack of dance partners. And as he studied her, she bit her lower lip as if biting back a retort. All of a sudden, he realized she might have misinterpreted his words. "What I mean to say is that I am disappointed that your father is not present. I was hoping to meet him and—"

"I understand you perfectly, Your Grace." A frosty tone edged her voice. "No need to explain."

He had upset her. *Badly done.*

An awkward silence surrounded them as the set ended and people mulled about once more. Lady Elizabeth and Stanhope returned and dispiritedness washed over him. Eager to gain an audience with her father and put this prickly reunion behind them, he asked, "May I have the next dance?"

Lady Elizabeth clasped Lora's hands, then glanced up at him expectantly. Lora, however, seemed unapproachable.

Recognizing their confusion, and how ludicrous he appeared, he breached the divide. "It would be a great honor to dance with both of you, but I confess to addressing Lady Lora at present."

Lady Elizabeth's smile waned as Lora quickly came to her defense. "My friend dances far better than I, Your Grace. Perhaps—"

"Are you otherwise engaged?" he asked, detouring her rejection.

Lady Elizabeth bent to whisper in Lora's ear. The latter's expression altered significantly. She searched the room, a battle waging war behind her eyes. "Very well."

She held out her gloved hand, and he took it, her flawless skin brightening as she smiled and he led her to the dance floor. Filled with a sense of calm, he placed her fingers in the crook of his elbow, feeling more alive than he could remember and wondering at the change in himself. Her touch sent a charge through his extremities, instantly trans-formative, and far more destructive to his plans than he'd ever imagined possible.

Warily, he reset his goals. He hadn't attended Putney's house party to form an attachment to Lora or anyone else, as much as she'd haunted his dreams. He had a mystery to solve and a killer to catch.

But what had Lady Elizabeth whispered in Lora's ear?

Had she reminded Lora that refusing to dance when asked prevented a lady from dancing with anyone else? Possibly. But he'd never known a young woman to actually summon such criticism. Truth be told, no female he'd ever seen had refused to dance with him, especially spurred on by match-making mamas with visions of grandeur.

But he sensed Lora desired to. Why? *I am kind and polite, wealthy and wise. Tall, handsome, and dedicated. No woman has ever avoided me before.* And wasn't this house party an opportunity to broker a betrothal for her? Stupefied, he licked his wounded pride as dancers parted to provide them space.

The waltz began.

He gazed down at Lora's indifferent expression, laboring over the exhilarating challenge she presented. *Remember, old boy, you need an audience with the marquess, nothing more.* Lora's future nuptials were none of his business.

Ignoring the friction flaring between them, he chose a suitable topic to break the ice. "My compliments to whoever arranged the exquisite décor. The attention to detail exceeds my expectations."

"And what, exactly, did you expect to find when you arrived, Your Grace?" She cocked her head to the side, studying him. "Would you have us believe country dances pale in comparison to city balls? Are we not as established and genteel?"

"You misunderstand." He spun her around in dizzying circles. "No matter the expense or location, every ball is a tedious chore."

Her eyes narrowed. "Then why attend at all?"

I seek answers. "It is my present desire to—" he started without thinking, about to say *'make amends.'* "In regards to Winterbourne, it is my understanding the marquess has recovered and—"

"You are two years too late," she said, quickly cutting him off.

"Too late?" Shock shot through him. Inconceivable as it was, the marquess's long road to recovery and his absence from the House of Lords had caused many to worry that something untoward had occurred. "But your father is alive, is he not?"

"He is."

Their gazes locked, hers combative, his probing. He felt tension seize her spine as she pulled away from his embrace. *Blood and hounds!* Why did he feel she wanted to avoid conversation about her father altogether? "His injuries—"

"Were severe, Your Grace. But this is a ball, is it not? Why ruin the ambiance with topics that occasion pain?"

Bollocks! Every word coming out of his mouth seemed offensive to her. "I believe we have gotten off on the wrong foot."

"Your Grace." After an audible pause, she added, "You are an excellent dancer. And this is a ball where flights of females constantly besiege titled gentlemen. If you are unhappy with my expertise, or lack of it, another lady will surely satisfy."

The realization that he didn't want to dance with anyone else hit him hard. He fancied Lora, had always desired her. But in this instance, he wanted what she could provide—an audience with her father. And it was imperative that he got one. "Finding another partner won't be necessary. I would not want to subject you to undue criticism."

She stomped on his foot, meeting his stare with incomparable resolve. "How about now?"

"You little minx." He glanced around and discovered they were under close scrutiny. Pulling her close, he whispered in her ear. "I wouldn't want you to embarrass yourself in front of your guests."

"Why have you come . . . after all this time?"

He detected a tremor in her voice, so he said simply, "Kingston is my home."

"Something you seemed to have forgotten until now."

"I didn't forget." He spun her back into his embrace and their gazes locked in a clash of wills that energized his blood. "I know what I want."

"And what, pray tell, could that be?" she asked.

"The answer may surprise you."

"How so?" she asked doe-eyed, a hint of mischief and madness glinting behind her crooked spectacles.

"Has distancing yourself from Society blinded you?" He longed to make her understand that if she'd finished the Season, he could have shown her that she was the only woman for him. *Liar!* He'd been dead set on avoiding the ball and chain, and had been relieved when she no longer posed a temptation. "How long since you last visited London?"

"You are transparent, Your Grace."

He sucked in a breath, wondering if she had the ability to read minds. "Am I?"

"You have deftly maneuvered the conversation back to my father."

He exhaled a sigh of relief. "Indeed, I have."

He led her around the dance floor, noting a particular veteran smirked whenever they passed. *Lieutenant Samuel Hawkesbury.*

"Your Grace, I fail to understand why it is so important for you to meet my father. Can your business not wait until the morrow?"

"No. But it seems I do not have a choice in the matter." To circumvent an unwelcome confrontation with the lieutenant, Myles swept Lora to the other side of the ballroom. "*'The existence of things depends on their being perceived'*, Lady Lora."

"So, you are a philosopher." She recognized Berkeley. That was a surprising revelation. Most women did not find reading about the principles of human knowledge particularly entertaining. "Well, I observe a great many things, too, Your Grace." Daggers shot from her eyes. "Do not fault me for donning armor. Like others of my sex, circumstances have forced me into the battle."

"Being suitably armed is a wise choice." She had much to lose in the matter of who would inherit when her father died. "Accept my condolences. The situation that you and your father find yourselves in is not ideal. I never had a brother, but I know, based on your devotion, that yours must have been a good man."

"He was, Your Grace." Emotion brightened her eyes in the candlelight. "Do not speak any more of it, I beg."

He refused to let go, however, sparked by suspicion and a niggling desire to soothe her. She'd suffered unbearably, enduring her father's withdrawal from Society and her brother's death. "Life has not been easy for you, has it?"

"Clarify *easy*." Bold and brave, she met his stare.

He swept her around the room once more, keeping time to the music. Mindful that the lieutenant watched their every move, he quickly sought to turn her mind away from the morbid thoughts occupying the conversation. "Tell me about your home."

"Winterbourne?"

"No." *Fiend seize it!* They were not just waltzing in circles; they were talking around each other. And, by Jove, he was making a muck of it. "Kingston," he said, "the birthplace of England. Where King Egbert and Archbishop Ceolnoth joined forces, and seven Saxon Kings—Edward the Elder, Athelstan, Edmund, Edred, Edwig, and Ethelred—were crowned on the coronation stone, now mounted outside the town hall."

"You know your history. Surprising, given how long you have been in Town."

He ignored the rib. "Of course, I know my history." They danced past Lieutenant Hawkesbury again. The man quickly snapped to attention and pretended to converse with someone to his left when Myles caught him staring. "My lengthy time away puts me at a great disadvantage. As it happens, I am keen to learn about the area and its *inhabitants.*"

"Why?"

Her question was innocent enough, so he produced the first answer that came to his head. "I *am* the Duke of Beresford."

Producing a winning smile, he expected a swoon, but the giddy reaction did not come. Strange. His ability to charm the most withered of wallflowers had never failed him before. Was he losing his touch?

"Perhaps the information you seek would be more forth-coming if you entertained a lasting fascination for *your* birthplace."

"Lasting—" He fought the urge to describe what Kingston meant to him, and the death stare that haunted him still. *Stuart.* She could not understand the horror and guilt plaguing him. She ought not. Why, mere hours ago, they'd put his faithful servant to rest. "I have . . . obligations."

Her glistening lips summoned him like a shimmering lure. "I am a woman, Your Grace. What are duty and obligation to me?"

The last chord of the waltz played, the strains hovering before fading away. Separating, they stared at one another before Lora frostily curtsied, then departed, immediately followed by her first cousin.

Irked by Hawkesbury's endeavors to occupy Lora's attention, Myles sought out Stanhope. Amid fluttering fans and murmuring gossip, he wove through the crowded room to

Hawkesbury the elder. The man appeared to be conversing with the solicitor about some serious matter.

Had word got out about the robbery at Darby and Stuart's death? He'd sworn his entire staff to secrecy. Servants talked, however. It was only a matter of time before half the countryside feared for their very lives. And the longer they maintained peace, the quicker they could restore safety.

Putney was out of reach for the time being. Lora held prejudice against him. But the Honorable Thomas Hawkesbury might prove to be a fount of information, especially when it came to his son. Grimes's paperwork divulged the extent of Lieutenant Hawkesbury's debts. They were great. Odd, that. Given that he'd supposedly been serving in military campaigns.

Was there a connection between Lieutenant Hawkesbury, Stuart's death, and the red-cloaked highwaywoman? He shook off the thought.

He knew one thing for certain. *'There is no greater tyranny than that which is perpetrated under the shield of the law and in the name of justice.'*

CHAPTER 6

"**Y**ou are the only fortunate female in the room," Eliza said. "You danced with the duke. Where is your enthusiasm? Tell me, what is he like?"

Lora rolled her eyes, fighting the mushrooming turmoil settling in her belly. "He . . . He—"

"Has left you speechless," Eliza said with sunny cheerfulness. "Well, isn't that something?"

"No. No. It is not what you think. He has shown no interest in me at all."

"That is not how it looked while you danced. He seemed determined to keep your attention."

"There you are correct," she admitted. "Although not for the reasons you suggest. He kept asking questions about Kingston, my father, and—"

"And?" Eliza asked, waiting expectantly.

"He offered his condolences for Nicholas's death."

"Is that all?" Eliza frowned. "How strange. From the way the two of you were looking at each other, I thought . . . Surely—"

"You thought wrongly."

A warm flush swept over Lora. She stroked her arm, recalling the duke's touch. He was a fine creature, finer than any she'd ever seen in her entire existence. His physical attributes had undergone significant alteration. He was taller in stature, with blond hair and blue eyes. A complete contrast of light to her dark. Indeed, he exuded calm authority, a take-charge-attitude that promised guidance to her worn spirit.

"He is the spitting image of his father," Eliza concluded. "I always thought the old duke was a handsome man. Though he was much too old for me."

"Eliza!"

"Old. Young." Her friend pouted. "What does it matter? I do not intend to be a burden to my parents."

"Have your mother and father ever led you to believe that you are a burden?"

"No," Eliza said wistfully. "But we all universally acknowledge that the eldest should marry first. With two sisters waiting in the wings, it is my duty to marry soon."

"Nobody is guaranteed love." Aunt Meg's hopes for her jumped to the forefront of Lora's mind. Marriage brought security and the added bonus of sweet little babes for her aunt to coddle. Pining for love set off a carillon of alarm for any wallflower. "No matter how hard we may wish for it, we cannot control Fate."

Eliza chuckled. "I will take matters into my own hands if need be."

"Take care, Eliza," she warned her friend. Lora had done things, said things, witnessed the unthinkable, and continued to take matters into her own hands. Where had it gotten her? She still didn't know who the man with the orange neckerchief was, who he worked for, or where he would strike next, and that was a constant frustration. "Be careful what you wish for."

"We are wallflowers, Lora. Wishes and dreams are all that we have."

Her gaze strayed to the Duke of Beresford, who stood out, dressed in a sea of black and cream, with his white linen stock and neatly tied cravat. During the waltz, his searching eyes had delved deep into her soul, stripping away the barriers necessary to hide her innermost secrets. "Being a wallflower is not the end of the world."

Beresford's attention was. His presence made her heart drum violently in her chest. His nearness jeopardized her cause. The attack on her defenses was a shock so rare, so sensual and seductive and strong, it brought to mind the first time she'd seen the then Lord Rutland, fresh out of Oxford, and waited for him to sign her dance card. *He never did.* She'd almost never recovered from the cut direct. But he was here, now, a young duke of renown, coming in all his state to confuse and charm her. Certainly, the threat he posed to the role she played—that of a mild-mannered wallflower with a saddled nose—disrupted her plans to avenge her brother and heightened the risk that her mask might slip. Being distracted frightened her more than moonless nights, armed bandits, and crossbow pikes.

Then there was this disorderly twinge in her belly. Whenever he looked her way or came near, the earth rocked beneath her feet. Oh, he was dangerous, all right. And someone needs to intervene before the ground gives away, opening and deepening ruts, and trapping her in a flood of passion in the mire.

"What I object to," Eliza complained, "is this unbearable waiting. What I wouldn't give to be able to ask a man to dance."

"I do not think the *ton* will ever allow that." She laid her gloved hand on her friend's arm. "Hoping for miracles is a waste of time."

"Balderdash!" Eliza snapped her fan closed, a flash of humor crossing her face. "We do not need miracles. You and I are just as accomplished as any other female in this room. And you are the daughter of our esteemed host."

"Shhh." She played a game of cat and mouse. No one could discover that she was the cloaked woman in the woods. One wrong word or look might draw suspicion her way. "I do not desire attention."

Beresford had caught her once.

He could do it again.

Would she be able to escape a second time?

No. The less she and the duke had dealings, the better.

"Honestly, I do not understand you. Your aunt took great pains to arrange this house party, but you act like you want no part of it."

"That isn't necessarily true. You are here." She flashed a winning smile to cheer Eliza's spirits. "And I will feel doubly blessed if my father summons the strength to attend." She worried her bottom lip. "The exposure to people would do him good. If only—"

"The duke knew how much you adore him," Eliza said with a sigh.

"No." Fear seized her. "He can never find out. I would die of sheer mortification."

Among other things. The world she traversed would cease to exist if the duke found out that she was in love with him. People would place expectations upon her. More eyes would watch her every move. Besides, he hadn't accepted the invitation to Winterbourne to find a wife, and she had no need for a husband . . . yet.

Despite everything, Eliza persisted and wouldn't be put off. Opening her fan, she stepped forward and shielded their faces. "Be honest. You desire him still."

"Eliza." She glanced around to make sure no one overheard them. Beresford's reasons for attending their little house party were personal and grievous, and the questions he brandished were far more dangerous. "I have outgrown such fantasies, and he has left Society to take his father's place. He desires to know the area, its people, that is all."

"I doubt he danced with you in order to get information that can be easily obtained from any man of our acquaintance. No," Eliza said, smiling. "The tension between the two of you clearly hinted at something more while you were dancing."

"You are wrong. I should be happy never to see the duke again." *Liar!* Strength and power were seductive forces. One word from Beresford could put everything to rights. He had connections. He could hire men, locate Nicholas's killers, and put them to the noose. *But then I would not have the satisfaction of watching the life fade from my enemy's eyes.* "Besides, I cannot marry until Papa has fully recovered. No, indeed. I assure you I am not under the duke's spell."

"That is not what I saw."

Smothering a groan, she hugged her friend close, hating the need for dishonesty. Until Nicholas's death, she had withheld nothing from Eliza. However, times had changed. If Eliza knew what she was up to, she would quickly put an end to her schemes out of concern for her safety.

"Your eyes only see goodness and that is why I adore you," she said. "You restore balance and beauty to the world and keep it from feeling like a dismal place."

"Oh, Lora. Though we may occasionally be blind to it, I truly believe that goodness exists. Worthy souls attract happiness." Eliza affectionately gripped her hand. "Even piqued wallflowers."

She chuckled at Eliza's play on words. "You are a bright star. Truly wonderful and wise."

"I tell myself that every morning." Eliza managed a small,

tentative smile. "When I stand before the looking glass, mind you. But . . . this is my third season." She covered her mouth, mocking the absurdity. "Forgive me for mentioning it again. I know that personal matters have kept you from coming to London, and you have experienced more suffering than anyone should have to endure. But other than Mr. Stanhope, I fear—"

"Nothing." She squeezed Eliza's hand, ignoring the torrent of emotion flooding her heart. Self-pity contributed naught to one's plight other than making a person the most miserable of souls to be around. And a ball was not the place to snivel and whine, even in Samuel's presence. "The only interest required to sustain you, Eliza, should be your own."

"That is not the same thing, Lora, and you know it." Eliza trained misty eyes on the dancing bodies moving across the ballroom floor. "I want marriage and babies—"

"And you shall have them," she assured her. Even she had those earnest desires, though they hung to be pecked to the bone like Jerry Abershawe's corpse.

No one married a felon. Fine gentlemen—her liberal description of vandals of female virtue—preferred fluttering fans, coy glances, and secret interludes to the qualities that enhanced a woman's appeal; talents for something other than breeding. She was a marquess's daughter, encouraged to marry within her station. The aristocracy limited her choices, though that pool also included dandies and droll politicians, none of whom would be interested in marrying a woman destined to be hanged.

"Don't look now." Eliza gestured to the doorway. "He is coming."

"Who?" Suddenly perplexed, she searched the ballroom floor, half-expecting and dreading to see the duke approach for another dance.

"Your cousin."

Her inner turmoil heightened, her head swirling with doubt. "Do not stare. That will only encourage him."

"I shall persuade him to ask me to dance," Eliza said, fluttering her fan. "I will rid you of him in a thrice."

"Do nothing of the sort, Eliza," she hissed. "He is not a trustworthy man."

But it was too late. Unaware of the danger, Eliza pretended to look besotted, earning Samuel's broad smile as he approached, forcing Lora to reluctantly admit that her cousin appeared handsomely turned out in his regimentals. Lieutenant Samuel Hawkesbury presented himself to all and sundry as a hero, and luxuriated in the resulting praise. *Nauseating.* Unless war had dealt him a jarring reality and transformed the tyrant, she'd bet her life that his soul was still as black as the dead of night.

He drew closer, unmistakable derision radiating from his eyes, quickly putting to rest any ideas of alteration. His smug disdain for others stirred her instincts, warning her to stay on her guard. From his hessians to his lean, lithe figure, to his broad-shouldered epaulettes, high stock and perfectly tied cravat, it appeared the militia recommended the spiteful brat who'd vowed to make her regret rejecting him.

"Lady Lora." Her cousin's dignified air and his mockingly suave bow assaulted her senses.

Watched by a gaggle of witnesses, she dipped a quick curtsy. "Lieutenant."

"Come now. Are we not family? Surely, after all this time, you will use my given name. We Hawkesburys are immune to formality, are we not?"

"You are correct in one regard. It has been a long time." *Not long enough.*

She detected a twitch in his lower lip before his attention shifted to Eliza. "And who is this lovely confection by your side?"

"Do you not remember?" Instinct advised against introductions, but decorum prevailed. "Lady Elizabeth. This is my cousin, Lieutenant Samuel Hawkesbury."

"We have met previously, though you may not remember, as it was five years ago." Performing an elegant curtsy, Eliza added, "How do you do?"

"Lady Eliza," he said, infuriating Lora by using her friend's nickname. "A woman grown. You are a delight in this veteran's eyes. The pleasure is mine, I assure you." Yielding another gallant bow, he brought Eliza's hand to his lips, then peered at Lora with contrived importance and an indecent amount of tomfoolery. "Forgive me. I could not help but notice you from across the room. If you are not otherwise engaged, may I request to have my name written on your dance card?"

The dye cast, Eliza's wide-eyed enthusiasm sealed her fate. "M-My card?" she falsely stuttered.

"The very one." His broad, slithery smile rippled through Lora like an advancing tide, filling her with multiple misgivings. Given all that had occurred between them in their youth—the competition and jealousy—she had good reason to harbor distrust for her cousin. In truth, the sensation consumed her entire being for far stronger reasons than she could fathom. But were her assumptions wrong? Festooned with military honors, Samuel's uniform practically gleamed with pageantry. She had to consider whether it was possible that he had come home a different man, given that war had changed men for better or worse. "I would be honored to have the next waltz."

"As would I." Eliza's sigh ground through Lora's ears. If her friend didn't tone down her feminine wiles, Samuel would quickly catch on.

"Delightful. Only Lady Eliza just mentioned that she needed a drink. We were just about to—"

"Is that so?" Samuel bared his teeth, bent near, and whispered something only Lora could hear. "Be a good girl and get your friend a drink, and have it waiting for her when the music ends, eh? And while you're at it, see that my father gets something to drink too. He looks pale, if you ask me."

Alarmed, she shot a look at her uncle. From across the room, he appeared to wobble but was quickly put to rights by the man at his side. By the time she recovered from what she'd seen and sought out Eliza, her friend produced a theatrical parting smile.

Oh, Eliza. What have you done? It never boded well to encourage Samuel.

She watched their retreating figures and wondered how far Samuel would go to get what he wanted. Would he hurt her blameless friend to get back at her as he'd done so often with innocent animals or the tenants on the estate?

"Lady Lora, are you unwell? You look as if you've seen a ghost."

Startled from her nightmarish musings, she cast a worrisome glance at the tall man who appeared at her side. Oh, why did the duke have to be so handsome? His chiseled brow and sculpted jawline housed the finest set of lips she'd ever seen, setting her heart aflutter. "You are mistaken. I was speaking briefly to my cousin."

"I've been told some men are returning from Waterloo behaving like ghosts of themselves."

Heartbreaking. In Samuel's case, however, she knew he would never put himself in harm's way. He was a coward, through and through. "My cousin appears unchanged."

"That, too, can be detrimental. If I have learned anything in my sessions in parliament, it is this. A man hides many faces."

A woman does too. "Are you suggesting that Samuel is hiding something?"

"Only you can answer that. I do not know the man."

I have every reason not to trust him. She flipped open her fan to cool the flush creeping into her face, desiring to hide any emotion she might unwittingly expose at the mere mention of her cousin. "What is there not to know? His embellishments are there for all to see, Your Grace."

He cleared his throat. "I did not come to interrogate you. You have my word as a gentleman. Rather, I came to apologize."

"What do you have to apologize for, Your Grace?"

He peered at her intently. "My previous conduct."

"I suspect it is I who should apologize to you." She fanned her face faster. She regretted jumping to conclusions, but she would never regret his touch, his nearness, or his leather and sandalwood scent. She met his stare, feeling an unreasonable desire to unburden herself of these feelings for reasons which beggared belief. "You have not offended me, nor do I believe you are capable of doing so. It takes a great deal more than a dance to bend my will."

An instant wistfulness stole his expression. "Be that as it may, allow me to explain."

She nodded, hesitantly. "Very well."

He shifted on his feet and searched the crowd where friends and acquaintances mingled, his size making it unlikely he missed a thing taking place. "There is . . . That is to say—"

"Oh!" she exclaimed, a sudden urge to shift the conversation gripping her like a vise. "It just occurred to me that I have neglected to offer my condolences, Your Grace."

Raucous laughter and snatches of music filled the air, a stark contrast to the serious turn of their conversation. "You heard?"

"News of this nature is hard to conceal, especially in Kingston." He, of course, alluded to the death of his butler, but she did not. Rather, she intended him to believe that she was offering condolences for his father's death. She clutched her neck, assuming a look of innocence, at odds with herself for tricking him into revealing what he knew about the thieves who tried to break into his home. "Since your brief return for your father's funeral, I have not had the opportunity to extend my sympathies and—"

"You misunderstand, Lady Lora."

She had him. "What is there to misunderstand?"

The look he gave her filled her with dread. "So, you have not heard."

"Heard, what? Is there something I should know? Has something happened to threaten our gathering?"

He led her to a potted palm. "There is no easy way to say this. Thieves broke into my estate several nights ago."

Wearied by indecision, she asked, "Was anyone harmed?"

"Yes." Muscles ticked in his jaw as he studied her. "Stuart, my butler, did not survive."

She no longer had to pretend. The sounds of the wood, the hunt, the urgency of that night flooded back, reminding her how fragile life was.

"No." The word barely escaped her mouth before guilt overwhelmed her. Thankfully, the duke attributed her distress to the murder. He escorted her to a nearby chair and sat down beside her. "How?" she asked, fearing the blame he would undoubtedly lay at her feet.

"I did not mean to upset you with this news, Lady Lora. I only speak of it to warn you that the countryside isn't safe. To understand why, I am determined to learn as much as I can about the area and its people."

"I am terribly sorry about your butler. Had he been in your employ long?"

"Most of my life. Stuart dedicated himself to my father, but he also meant a great deal to me."

"What happened to him?"

"Perhaps I shouldn't discuss this. I do not want to frighten you."

"I must know," she insisted.

He breathed in a long breath. "Upon my recent return from London, I arrived to find my estate in chaos. Staff were scrambling to search the woods for thieves that had broken into the house. Later, I discovered that Stuart had been stabbed while trying to stop them."

"Did he suffer terribly . . . in the end?"

"I cannot say."

A tight knot within her begged for release. "Was she able to tell you who stabbed him?"

"No. But I almost caught one villain," he said grimly.

She pressed on, eager to find out what he knew. "What did this *villain* look like?"

"She rode a white horse and wore a red cloak."

"She?" Her composure nearly cracked. *Good God! He blames me for his butler's murder!*

"Yes." He rose in one fluid motion. "She will not be easy to trap, but capture her, I shall."

She raised her fan, swallowing with difficulty.

Samuel desired Nicholas's inheritance. She wanted to avenge Nicholas. And the duke plotted to unveil her identity.

What was she to do?

CHAPTER 7

*S*everal days after the ball, Lora folded a missive describing another murder of a local laborer. The details sent tremors through her, piercing her with regret. Unable to sleep, she snuck out to the stables and saddled her mount. Aided by a trickle of moonlight, she traversed the road to the village, shaking off the chill. Or was it a guilty conscience?

If not for a house full of guests and obligations, she might have been able to prevent Mr. Hobbs's death. If she had caught the bandits sooner, perhaps even the duke's butler might still be alive. She had been there, near the duke's lush estate. Upon hearing the shouts, she'd chosen not to enter the house and instead gave chase, fearing that she would be caught in a place where she was not supposed to be. In the end, fear of being blamed for whatever tragedy had befallen the household had gripped her so cruelly that when she spotted the duke in the woods, she'd instantly frozen.

If only she hadn't seen *him*. Perhaps then she might have caught the man in the orange neckerchief, and made a difference in the lives of so many others. But she hadn't. The fear of discovery had overshadowed her good sense, and that momentary pause had cost her the culprits responsible for the duke's butler's death.

Guilt-ridden, she reaffirmed her oath to catch the person responsible for all the nefarious goings on in Kingston. The dreadful events that had started with her family now extended to the village and called for drastic measures.

Time to put an end to this suffering.

She rode on, surrounded by nightly sounds that had become as ordinary as a cocking rooster waking the world. Bats foraging under the forest canopy, clicking as they darted in and out of the trees; badgers snuffling in the undergrowth and scuttling along; nightjars, seldom seen but heard, their cries carrying hundreds of yards. Legend said that the nocturnal birds were the spirits of unbaptized children, doomed to wander the night sky singing "Whip-poor-will." Joining their *chonk, chonk, chonk* cacophony were eager owls, croaking frogs, and the trickling rush of a woodland spring or the crack of wood snapping with the strain.

A woman's scream charged the air, bringing her to a halt.

Not ordinary.

She listened for the shrieking sound again. It could be a red fox or human; the two were hard to distinguish from the other.

There!

A cry louder than the first, and from something much larger. Prodding her horse into action, she raced down the London Road. Stealth and surprise, techniques mastered on hunts with her father and brother, were useless now. Speed was necessary.

Blood pounded between her ears, the cadence keeping time with horses' hooves clomping over the packed earth. Voices—a man, two women—drifted through the woods. She slowed her mount to a walk and rounded a bend in the trees, easing back on the reins when she espied the developing scene before her.

Draw.

Retrieving an arrow from her quiver, she silently slid from the saddle to creep closer.

A carriage stood vacant in the middle of the road, the door wide open. Two unwilling souls labored for freedom alongside a dark figure who fought to control them. One woman lost her footing, her gown tangling about her feet. She tumbled to the ground with a yelp.

Obscenities filled the air. "I told ye to give me yer valuables and be quick about it."

"We have nothing," she cried as the blackguard grabbed a fistful of her hair and yanked her to her knees. "Run, Ruth!"

Ruth launched an attack instead. "Don't 'urt my mistress!"

"I will do whatever I please, wench." Menacing laughter sent chills up Lora's spine as the blackguard turned, struck Ruth, and sent her careening to the ground.

Nock.

In a seamless transfer of energy, Lora placed the piece in the middle of her bowstring and stretched the serving, making her aim true so as not to hit the poor suffering woman in the man's clutches.

"She has nothin' of value to me," the blackguard said, focusing on his captive. "Ye're what I want."

Loose.

Releasing a breath, she let her weapon fly and, moving with swift patience, she nocked another and inched closer.

The man's reaction was swift as the arrow penetrated his thigh. He fell to the ground, cradling his leg. "Bloody hell!"

"Help us!" His captive scurried on her hands and knees to her traveling companion, sobbing. "Please, whoever you are, help us!"

Lora wasted no more time. She rushed to the woman's

side, brandishing her weapon and making it clear to the injured bandit she was not above sending another arrow through his rotten heart. "Do not move," she said, looking him over and searching for the telltale orange neckerchief that wasn't there. "I brought your arse to anchor once. The next time, it'll be your skull."

"Don't kill me. I meant no 'arm," he spat. "I was just—"

"Having a wee bit of sport?" she asked, trying to keep her anger in check.

"Aye, truer than not." He groaned, blood oozing between his fingers. "I seen the carriage pass and thought I'd 'ave a bit of fun with 'em. No 'arm done, eh?"

"No harm done?" the hurt woman wailed. She glanced at Lora, her red-rimmed eyes full of fright and fury. "This . . . this—"

"Bandit." She opened the lower decks, intending her insults and barbs to belittle and bedevil the man with a hang-gallows look. "A belly-gut, bacon-faced bastard. Blast him!"

"Yes." The injured woman struggled to her feet, favoring her side. "This blaggard chased our carriage, incapacitating our driver. Poor man, wherever he is now."

"Where is he?" She kicked the wounded man, but he refused to answer.

The woman quickly exclaimed, "I do not know where our driver is. Perhaps—"

"No," she said, stopping her from continuing on. She aimed her arrow at her attacker's most cherished parts. "Speak or bid your seed farewell."

"No, no, no." He raised his hand to ward off the liquidation of his worldly goods. "If it's the driver yer after, I shot 'im."

The bowstring clicked as she maximized her aim, summoning as much patience as she could muster.

"I don't think I killed 'im."

"If he is dead, he wouldn't be the first, I wager." She cast the woman a warning look when she ventured near to spit on the man, then gave him her full attention. "You are not from around here. How long have you been in Kingston?"

He glanced at his leg, then asked, "Are ye goin' to finish me?"

"You'll be a diet for worms on a dunghill if you don't answer my question. And I will get an answer." She placed her foot on his thigh, applying pressure to his wound. "Why are you here? Tell me!"

He shrieked like a pig. "To get . . . what's mine."

"Louder. One of your victims can't hear."

"To get . . . what's mine!"

"And what—"

"Please," the gentlewoman said, moving to rouse her companion. "The sight of this man sickens me, and my maid needs our help."

Lora stiffened, momentarily ashamed. "Get into the carriage," she ordered, turning toward the women. "I shall take you to safety shortly. But there is something I must do first."

"Are you going to kill him?"

While she was distracted, the thief swiftly rose, astonishing her with his speed, and rushed towards her. Instinctively, she let her arrow fly. It hit its target, impaling the man's chest. He slumped to the ground, gurgling.

The two women screamed.

"Get Ruth into the carriage," she ordered.

"You fool!" Dropping to her knees, she shook the highwayman none too gently. "I was going to let you live."

He gulped. "It was ye or me."

"Why are you terrorizing the area?" Tears of rage welled in the backs of Lora's eyes as the futility of what she'd done hit her. He was her one and only chance to get the answers she sought. "Did you kill the duke's man?"

"Wasn't me. Was—"

"Who?"

"It was—" He choked, the sound ominous in the night, the urgency nauseatingly real.

If she didn't find out who the man in the orange neckerchief was, she feared she'd never learn the truth.

"Clyde."

"Where is he? Where can I find him?"

"Smart one . . . 'e is."

Blood oozing out of the man's chest made her stomach churn. "And what about you? Why do this?"

Life waned from his eyes. "Blunt . . . to be earned—"

"For what?" She shook him again hard when he appeared to drift into the murky abyss. "Tell me!"

"Debts . . . London . . . Easy pickens, 'e said."

"Whose debts?"

The man's chuckle sounded vacant. "Luck . . . out."

"Where can I find Clyde?" she shrieked, becoming more desperate as the seconds wore on.

"He'll find . . . ye."

"He'll find me?" She blinked. "How will I know him?"

"Orange . . . neck . . ."

The blood siphoned from her face. "Neck? What about an orange neck?" She shook him harder. "Tell me!"

"Argh!" he growled, slowly reviving. His agony latched onto the woman in her, but being close to finding Nicholas's killer superseded everything else—including civility. "Penniless . . . promised."

Sounds of the forest quieted as horses' hooves thundered in the distance.

Time had run out.

With discovery imminent, she knelt down and hissed in

the man's ear. "If you live long enough, tell your master I'm coming for him."

Standing, she turned to the carriage; her cloak sweeping around her. She ran to her horse and brought him back to the conveyance, securing him to the boot, then climbed onto the box and took up the reins. Snapping them and shouting, "Move on," she raced off, putting as much distance between the coach and her pursuers as possible.

Several intense moments later, she took the carriage down the drive leading to one of her tenant's properties. There, she swiftly removed the brace of pistols at her hips, her bow and quiver, and tore off her cloak, setting them aside. She picked up a hat the driver had left lying on the box seat and plonked it on her head. From there, she continued on to Winterbourne's stables, their arrival causing instant upheaval.

Judson, the stablemaster, marched out holding a lamp aloft and shouting orders before rushing to her aid. "My lady," he said, recognizing her, "what the devil is goin' on?"

She gathered her belongings and lowered herself to the ground. "I couldn't sleep and went for a night ride."

He gawked as she passed off her accoutrements to a waiting stableman. "In a hired carriage?"

"It's a long story."

"One worth 'earin'." He drew closer. "If I'd known ye required a mount, I would 'ave sent one of the stable 'ands with ye. It isn't safe to be out alone. Not after—"

"We will talk about this later." There was no time to go into the details of what had occurred, and Judson would only worry more if he knew. She moved to the carriage doors and opened them, revealing the two frightened women huddled inside. "A highwayman accosted these ladies and they need immediate attention."

Acknowledgement transformed Judson's face.

"Bring them to the main house and provide them with the best of care."

"But ye're guests."

"These ladies are our guests. They just arrived late," she said calmly.

"But there will be—"

"It is nothing I cannot deal with," she insisted.

"No!" the unnamed woman cried out, her wide-eyed stare piercing Lora's heart. "This is all untoward. How do I know I can trust any of you?"

Judson spoke up for her. "My lady will not deal ye false."

"But how did we get here? And where is—"

"You are at Winterbourne, the Marquess of Putney's estate," Lora said, refusing to explain further.

"The Marquess of Putney?"

"Yes. The staff here will take good care of you. May I ask for your name?"

The woman hesitated, staring in disbelief, as if afraid to reveal her identity. "I am Wilhelmina Parr, and this is my maid, Ruth Finch."

"Miss Parr. Miss Finch. I am Lora, the marquess's daughter. I am sorry that we are meeting under these circumstances, but I am happy that you are alive. Please accept our hospitality, at least until my father's doctor can assure us that you are not in any danger."

"No," the unnamed woman said. "I do not wish you to go to any trouble on my account. Ruth and I shall be comfortable anywhere it is warm and dry."

"I will not hear of it." Lora gestured for the two women to exit the carriage, feeling outrage over how the man on the road had mistreated them. "The people of Kingston may be many things, but we are not heartless. Join us, I beg. Nay, I insist. Though I must warn you we are in the midst of a house party. Of course, I can arrange for your privacy." She recognized the worried expression marring Miss Parr's face. She'd seen that look on countless others who'd suffered horrifying cruelty at the hands of bandits, and it filled Lora with misgivings. "Rest assured, you will be safe here. And we will not expect you to mingle with our guests, at least not until you have recovered from your ordeal and wish it to be so."

"Very well." The bedraggled blonde beauty cried out when Judson attempted to guide her by the arm, making Lora recall the way they'd both been manhandled. Poor dears. "We accept," Miss Parr said. "For Ruth's sake."

"Then consider it settled," Lora said, celebrating this minor triumph.

What would have happened if she hadn't arrived in time? But she had and dared not ponder the alternative. Too many others had suffered worse at the hands of these men. These two ladies, in particular, were lucky, luckier than most. And now she knew more than she ever had about the man with the orange neckerchief.

Could it be that the moment for her to finally get revenge had come?

CHAPTER 8

$\mathcal{T}$he next morning, Lora came downstairs to break her fast, noting the late hour. Full sleep had never come, though she'd dozed at her desk while studying maps of the area. She replayed the altercation with the man on the road repeatedly in her head until she couldn't glean any more information, breaking down the encounter for clues where Clyde might take refuge.

Fingering her mourning ring, a lock of Nicholas's hair artfully braided and arranged within to form a heart, she fought back tears. No matter how close she came to exacting vengeance, nothing would bring her brother back.

How did one muster on when love seemed lost forever?

Entering the breakfast room, she was astonished to discover that Miss Parr and Miss Finch were already seated, despite having been given every impression that the two women did not want to be seen. They rose abruptly, as if caught doing something untoward.

"Miss Parr. Miss Finch." The two women exhibited social graces as curtsies were exchanged, making Lora believe they hailed from elevated Society. "What a surprise, and a pleasure to see you up and about this fine day. How are you faring? I admit that I did not expect to find you out and about so soon."

Miss Parr blushed and shot Ruth a glance. "Thank you for your concern, but there is no need to be alarmed."

"But surely, after what has happened, your health is an immediate concern. Has my father's surgeon examined you?"

"My lady—"

"Lady Lora, what Ruth means to say is that you are very kind," Miss Parr cut in. "And we take great joy in your hospitality. But that won't be possible. It would be unacceptable to distract the doctor from your father's care, let alone allow a strange man to evaluate my condition. You understand."

"I do not." Lora blinked. What reason could the woman have for being dead set against a doctor's care? "Dr. Wells is here daily, and Papa's needs are moderate. Allow him to examine you and ensure that, other than significant bruising, nothing has been overlooked. I insist." The silence that met her was palpable. Was Miss Parr concerned about being a burden and an inconvenience to their guests? "We are happy for you to remain at Winterbourne for as long as it takes to heal from your injuries. I assure you that you are welcome here."

"Thank you. We are in your debt, more than you know." Raising a cup of tea to her lips, Miss Parr peered out the double windows as if seeing something that wasn't there.

Lora nodded to a footman who poured her a cup of chocolate. "May I ask where were you headed before someone attacked your carriage, Miss Parr?"

"Mina." She lowered her teacup. "If we are to be friends, you must call me Mina."

Lora smiled, filled with an assurance that she was going to enjoy being around Mina immensely. "Mina. Then you must call me Lora. I shall hear of nothing less." *Now to tackle the problem head on.* Ruth looked extremely uncomfortable. Why? Was it because she sat at a nobleman's table and feared reproach? "While you are here, do not be troubled. I understand how hard it must be to rely on strangers."

Mina leaned across the table to clutch Lora's hand. "But we are not strangers, not anymore. What you have done—"

"And who do we have here?" Aunt Meg interrupted fortuitously upon entering the breakfast room at her normal time. A late riser, and her curiosity piqued, she did not mince words. "I do not recall meeting these two guests. Have they just arrived, Lora?"

"Late last night, in fact. Allow me to introduce Miss Wilhelmina Parr and Miss Ruth Finch. Difficulty on the road prevented them from arriving in time for the ball, Aunt."

"Oh, dear." Her aunt scrutinized the two women, and after a lengthy pause, said, "I hope you did not suffer the indignity of a loose wheel." Shuffling to a chair at the end of the table, her pristine skirts swishing about her, she waited for a footman to help her sit down. "Inoperative wheels take forever to rectify and often leave one standing in ankle-deep mud. Heavens! The very thought."

"No, Aunt." Lora smiled, hoping to ease Mina and Ruth's discomfort. She suspected distorting the truth agitated the two women. "It was not a loose wheel."

"Ah. Good news!" Meg nodded to the footman, who poured her a steaming cup of chocolate. "There is not much of that these days, except for the end of the war and Napoleon's well-deserved comeuppance. But with all of our countrymen returning and a lack of jobs waiting, things are . . . Well, nothing seems right." Her thoughts jumped to another topic. "Back to pleasantries. Where are you from?"

Here was a question even Lora wanted to know the answer to and waited expectantly to hear.

A forlorn smile flit across Mina's face. "Across the Thames."

"That is very vague." Meg set her teacup down. "That could be anywhere, East End, West End, Chelsea, Mayfair."

"Mina's wit is invigorating, is it not?" Lora laughed and nodded, encouraging Mina and Ruth to join her. "I always say that Chelsea continues to deprive us of each other's company. It's a pity that Mina's sister demands so much of her time. Oh, how I covet that precious bond." She glanced at her aunt, hating the lie but knowing the suggested attachment would win her aunt's sympathies. "I know you understand the extraordinary bond between sisters, Aunt."

Meg's eyes turned wistful. "How well, I do. A sister's love surpasses all." Gathering her emotions, she asked, "And you are unmarried, Miss Parr?"

"At the moment, yes."

Meg furrowed her brows. "What an odd answer."

But before her aunt could question Mina further, Lora's father ambled into the room, leaning heavily on his cane. He stopped almost as soon as he cleared the door and stared, dumbfounded, at the full table before him.

"Good morning, Papa." Lora left her seat to greet him and help him to his place at the head of the table.

"Forgive me," he said, taking in their new guests. "I thought most of our party had broken their fast and that the dining room would be empty."

"Nonsense," Meg said. "Join us at your leisure, my lord. It so happens we have the pleasure of entertaining new friends of Lora's acquaintance, Miss Parr and Miss Finch. Miss Parr. Miss Finch, the Marquess of Putney."

They exchanged courtesies.

Lora continued leading her father to the head of the table, where a footman eased him into his chair and retrieved his cane. All the while, she could not help but notice his attention kept straying to Mina. An involuntary reaction sent a swirling current of delight flowing through her. Why, if she wasn't mistaken, Papa could hardly take his eyes off Miss Wilhelmina Parr.

Could this be the miracle she'd been praying for?

Though Mina pretended not to notice, an instant spark ignited the room, producing cheerful smiles. Artless and serene eyes absorbed the moment, and Papa instantly regained his full, masculine laugh. The surprising interaction planted a seed in Lora's mind, furthering her hopes. Could Mina's arrival be the answer to their problems? She was young and unmarried, and Papa's spirits definitely benefited from her youthful presence.

Of course, it is too soon to contemplate marriage. None of them knew who Mina was or where she'd come from, or why she was traveling the road late at night without a proper chaperone. But, for the first time in a long time, hope blossomed in Lora's breast.

Until her cousin barged into the room, followed by the Duke of Beresford, and stopped cold. Several awkward moments later, Samuel placed his fowling piece against the wall. "Uncle, should you be up and about?"

Papa ignored Samuel's patronizing tone and instantly salvaged the mood as he rose. "Good day, Your Grace."

"Do not trouble yourself, Marquess," the duke quickly said, motioning for Lora's father to stay seated. "Not on my account. I am the one who is happy to finally obtain an audience with you."

The duke's calm consideration for his host was a stark contrast to Samuel's ill-bred haste. And to everyone's utter disbelief, Lora's cousin clomped to the sideboard in his gaiters, stuffed his plate, then plopped down in a chair next to her and began wolfing down his food.

She closed her eyes, praying for patience, before redirecting her attention to the duke, who still wore a double-breasted frock coat and carried his fowling piece. Mortified, she asked, "Did you enjoy your sport?"

"Yes, how was the hunt, Your Grace?" Papa's deepest regret was being unable to take part in the pastime. "I hope my gamekeeper brought out my prized pointers."

"They did a fine job of flushing out the grouse." He lifted his shotgun. "And I'm impressed with this piece. Is it from Davies Street?"

"I wouldn't go anywhere else," Papa said. "Manton is very reliable."

Lora's pulse suddenly leaped as he stroked the barrel. His powerful hands, masculine attire, and graceful movements were everything *The Sporting Magazine* suggested made for a superb hunter. "Astounding accuracy. I lost count at fifty."

Samuel stopped slurping his coffee to say, "Paget said I shot seventy-five."

"Join us, Your Grace." Lora pushed up her glasses and saddled her nose, conscious of keeping up appearances. "I am sure you must have worked up an appetite."

"Thank you." The look on the duke's face, however, implied that he would not accept. "I have something I need to attend to. There are matters I would like to discuss with you, Marquess, when you are available."

Papa quit the conversation he was having with Mina and gave the duke his full attention. "Of course. I shall be happy to meet you in my study in an hour's time, if that is acceptable."

"One hour then." Beresford nodded, then, turning to leave, stopped himself. "By the by, Hawkesbury told me that your brother has taken ill. I do hope that isn't the case. When last I saw him, he did not look well."

"Is that so, Samuel?" Papa asked.

"Yes." Samuel shrugged. "Come to think of it, Father hasn't been the same since I returned from the peninsula."

"Shouldn't you be with him?" Lora asked, shocked. "Have you informed Dr. Wells?"

Samuel dropped his spoon. "And miss all the fun? I have endured deprivation of every luxury for two years and barely survived Quatre Bras. My father has not. He can wait."

"Samuel!" Lora sputtered, bristling with indignation. "Do you think it was easy for your father, never knowing if you were dead or alive?"

He shrugged. Aunt Meg's nostrils flared, Mina paled, and Ruth stared at her lap. The duke cradled his fowling piece like he wanted to slam it over Samuel's head.

Papa released his pent-up breath. "Thank you for the information, Your Grace. I was unaware of my brother's condition. I will see that Dr. Wells pays him a visit posthaste."

How long had her uncle been sick? He'd been incredibly healthy all his life. With the safe arrival home of his son, what had changed?

That night, Lora sought escape from prying eyes at the whist tables. Spying two couples abandoning theirs, she commandeered an empty chair and picked up a stack of cards, pretending to be occupied.

While shuffling the deck and sorting her thoughts, Eliza joined her. "Lora, I have just heard the most shocking thing."

"What have you heard, Lady Eliza?" Before their conversation ever began, Samuel took a seat without asking permission. "I am always keen to hear the latest *on dits*. Broaden my horizons, won't you?"

Who invited him to play?

"May I join you?" The Duke of Beresford stood over them, dressed in a crisp tailored dark blue coat and matching breeches, and looking too handsome by half. "I see you have one spot left."

"You may, Your Grace," Lora said, trying to hide her frustration. Refusing the duke would only draw suspicion. Trapped between the two men in the world she desperately wanted to avoid, she prayed her mask did not slip. "Shall we?"

"Lady Eliza, it looks like you and I are in this together," Samuel said, reaching for the cards. "What say we make a wager against His Grace and Lora. Are you up for it?"

"Hold." Beresford warded off Samuel, the brush of his fingers sending a shiver through Lora's hand. "The lady can deal." The duke smiled, charm oozing out of every pore. "She has been shuffling the cards, if you require proof that the deck is ready."

How long had he been watching her? She wasn't sure how to process that information, whether to be frightened or relieved.

She passed the deck to Eliza, sitting to her right, and questioned the wisdom of being so close to the duke and under his intense scrutiny. Eliza cut the deck and handed it back.

Doling thirteen cards out to each player, Lora said, "Let's begin."

"What do you say to wagering a Crown per trick, and a guinea per Grand Slam?"

Beresford's eyes darkened dangerously. "This is not Brooke's, Lieutenant."

"And how I am glad of it," Eliza said, lightening the tone. "Else Lora and I would not be here."

"A half-penny per trick, then." Lora knew from paperwork in that cowardly solicitor's possession that Samuel could not afford to gamble. Far from it. For too long, Uncle Thomas had protected her cousin, paying off his creditors. And it was his lack of self-control that worried her most. How far was Samuel willing to go to inherit Winterbourne? And when he did, how long before he mortgaged it to the hilt? She dealt the last card to herself, turned it over, then placed it in the middle of the table. "Your trick."

"Spades," Samuel said, acknowledging the trump suit. He covered the ten with a King of Spades.

The duke played a two.

Eliza a six.

As Samuel gathered up his trick, the duke asked, "How is your father this evening?"

"Papa?" She lowered a five of hearts to the table. "He is well, thank you. I expect him to appear soon. In fact, against all odds, I do believe your presence has helped revive him. He's missed your father."

"As do I," he said.

Samuel laid down a Queen of Spades triumphantly.

Eliza gasped.

The duke peered at Lora over his hand, then dispatched an ace. "I suspect the credit for your father's improved health is not due to me, but to Miss Parr's presence."

"Miss Parr." Samuel flagged down a footman for a drink, and Eliza plonked a four on the table as Beresford gathered the trick he'd won. Drinking his champagne without apparently tasting it, her cousin asked, "Where the devil did Miss Parr come from?"

"It is all very mysterious," Eliza proposed.

Indeed. When Mina's arrival at Winterbourne had been explained without revealing too many details, Papa insisted on having the poor woman seen by Dr. Wells. Mina reluctantly agreed, and the good doctor was called back from Uncle Thomas's bedside to do a thorough examination. Thankfully, her injuries were limited to bruised ribs, and a sprained wrist—discomfort she had hidden from everyone, except her lady's maid. While Ruth refused to be explored, concealing the lump on her head with a cap. Dangerous considering that the devoted servant had lost consciousness on the London Road.

"Miss Parr has an indomitable spirit," Lora said, calling to mind the way she'd even pleaded for her attacker's life.

"I sense that as well." Eliza smiled broadly as she lowered a card. "And your father appears quite enamored with her."

"Nonsense," Samuel spat. "You exaggerate, surely."

"How so?" Lora asked, clenching her jaw. Papa's interest in Mina provided hope that he desired to live on. And, with it, came possibilities that another heir to the Marquess of Putney would be born. Though no one could ever take Nicholas's place, a newborn baby's cry filling these hallowed halls would replenish what Winterbourne had tragically lost. "You should know by now that my father is perfectly capable of making his own decisions."

"He is too old for her," Samuel snapped. "It's as simple as that."

"Says who?" Eliza asked. "From what I have observed, Miss Parr and the marquess are perfectly suited for one another."

"Don't be a fool." Samuel snatched another glass of champagne from a passing footman and downed the contents. "He's lame." His words were beginning to slur, making her wonder how much he had already imbibed. "Hardly able to pleasure a woman in—"

"Enough!" the duke said, drawing worried glances from the other whist tables as he bolted from his chair. "Are you aware that you have just insulted your host, and by proxy, his daughter?"

Lora rose, desperate to dispel the threat of violence hanging in the air. "Both of you are causing a scene."

"Careful, Your Grace," Samuel spat. "She bites."

Beresford cleared his throat. "Perhaps you should take your leave."

"Your Grace." A footman carrying a silver salver fortuitously saved the moment. "A missive has arrived for you."

The welcome distraction allowed everyone to take a much-needed breath. Curiously, she and Eliza and Samuel watched the duke break open the seal and read his letter.

After a few nerve-wracking seconds, he looked up.

"I hope you have received good news," she said, thankful for the interruption.

"Excellent news, in fact. The men I have assembled to locate my butler's killers are ready for action and are even now scouring the countryside for clues."

Lora's heart sank into her belly. If that was the case, the danger to her had increased tenfold.

"So, you have become Kingston's protector." Samuel smirked, daggers of disdain shooting from his eyes. "What, may I ask, has Lora done to earn your shield?"

She gasped. "Samuel!"

A muscle flicked angrily in the duke's jaw. "Apparently, you have been away from Kingston for far too long. Battlefield conduct is unacceptable in polite society. Take care, sir. You are not at war anymore."

"Am I not?" Samuel grabbed another glass of champagne, gulped it down, and slammed the stem on the table, surprisingly leaving it intact. "Another." He waved to onlookers, then said the most shocking thing. "I've seen things that would make your skin crawl." He chuckled at something he found amusing. "Though I owe my father a debt of gratitude for putting me in a position where I could visit the city frequently and receive an enthusiastic welcome. Town is quite diverting to a lonely officer."

"If you were with your regiment, how were you able to find time to visit Town?" Eliza innocently asked.

Samuel instantly paled. "Does a flower understand the sun, wind, and rain?"

"Apologize to Lady Lora and Lady Elizabeth for your boorish behavior," the duke demanded.

Lora knew what her cousin was capable of. He thrived on drama, always had. And she'd better put a stop to it before things got more out of hand than they already were. "Insults benefit no one. Perhaps a turn about the gardens and fresh air will clear your head, Samuel."

"You cannot expect me to go out there," he complained. "It. Isn't. Safe."

Her eyes locked with Beresford's. "What do you mean it isn't safe?" she asked, trying to calm him. "Did you not hear that the duke has employed men to patrol the area?"

"Have you not heard about the theft and murders taking place? It is dangerous out there, I tell you." He jerked his arm away from the duke, who'd come forward to escort him outdoors. Leaning toward her, he whispered in Lora's ear. "I will never forgive you for this."

"What have I done?" A nagging suspicion in the back of her mind refused to be stilled. Had he learned her secret? But that was impossible. Wasn't it? As she watched him stomp out of the parlor like a petulant child, she frowned nervously. What would Samuel do next? Something had triggered his alarm, whether it was the champagne, discussing the war, references to his father, the possibility of her father marrying again, or losing at cards. At the end of the day, her cousin did not like being inconvenienced. "Forgive him."

"I fail to understand your cousin's lack of decency, Lora. If you'll excuse me," Eliza said, drifting away from the table, leaving her alone with the duke.

"Are you well?" the duke asked before pressing on. "If I had known that conversing about his father would—"

"Think nothing of it. I am sure his father's poor health has been a strain. You and I can attest to that." But Samuel's discomfort had heightened at the mention of going outdoors. Which made little sense. Was something or someone out there the cause?

CHAPTER 9

$\mathcal{A}$ sennight after the party began, dewy splendor covered the lush green landscape. Winterbourne was a carefully tended estate of woodland trees bordering a lake and small flowering shrubs that accented every bend. An arched bridge and Grecian temple complimented the flora and fauna, befitting Georgian style, and were easily reached via a specific route meant to show off Brown's design to full effect, if one walked the circular path.

Lora stood on the verdant grass in a green nankeen coat trimmed in black over a pale-yellow gown, with matching gloves and kid-skin boots. Surrounded by a group of sport enthusiasts debating the distance between two archery targets set fifty yards apart—an allowance made for the women since men shot at one-hundred yards—Lora studied Eliza's form as her friend took aim then let the shaft fly.

"Drat!" A generous amount of applause endeavored to boost Eliza's spirits as the arrow landed on the board's outer rim. "Missed . . . again."

Several women gathered around Eliza to congratulate her for actually hitting the panel.

"You're mistaken." Lora had been training Eliza off and on for the past year. She came to stand beside her, hoping to encourage her. "Practice makes perfect. Every attempt is progress on the last, and you, dear friend, have improved."

Eliza's cheeks flushed, and she smiled past her embarrassment. "I wish I had as much confidence in my abilities as you do, Lora." She placed the bow on the stand set out for their use so that someone else could take a turn. "Perhaps I should stick to what I do best."

"And what is that?" Miss Parr sweetly asked.

"Reading."

The group was so busy laughing, they neglected to notice the duke's approach. "Fresh air and exercise are good for the soul, but mastering the mind . . . Now, that is the most challenging pastime of all. And if that brings you joy, Lady Elizabeth, your aim is true."

Lora couldn't believe her ears. Was the man a poet?

She hated to memorize poetry, but she respected a well-turned-out sportsman, especially one who chose not to hawk his skills. And what woman didn't? *Egads!* The duke looked resplendent in a dark-green coat trimmed in black, a fawn-colored waistcoat, and trousers, a white cravat, and knee-high black boots.

Before she could find her voice, a new one entered the fray. "Why would anyone want to closet themselves in a library when the best place for a woman to show off her figure to effect is on the field with a bow in her hand?" Cringing, Lora fought to ignore her crude cousin but, as usual, he made that task difficult. It was his opinion that women were not fit for sport unless flirting and mingling with men. To which she vehemently disagreed. "Do you shoot, Your Grace?"

"I do." Beresford took his time before being more descriptive. "But not to flirt or mingle with the ladies."

Samuel spoke before she realized her mouth hung agape. "Ah," her cousin said catching on. He snatched a bow from the table and shoved it at the duke with the type of force that suggested he did not appreciate being made a fool of. "Perhaps you will honor us with a display of your prowess then, eh? I, for one, am interested in the training you received at Eton. What say we place a bet on the outcome?"

"I do not think that is wise, Samuel." Why gamble with money he did not have?

"Far be it from me, cousin, to ruin your party with a meager bet." Samuel shot a look at Beresford, while Lora and Eliza and Mina looked on. "Or are you above the challenge, Your Grace?"

She grabbed hold of Samuel's arm, despising the way he'd pushed in on their fun and ruined the happy moment. "Samuel, stop. The duke is our guest."

People gathered round. Eliza backed away. Mina stared in disbelief as Lora watched, stunned. What lengths was her cousin willing to go to win a bet?

"He is a member of this party, is he not?"

"I am," the duke answered Samuel.

Mina whispered in her ear. "I know you could easily put him in his place."

"Shhh. No one can know the truth about how good I really am."

"But—"

"I would dearly love to put Samuel in his place, but it is imperative that you keep my secret. This is an opportunity for the duke to break away from his father's shadow. I cannot steal his thunder. Secondly, when it comes to my cousin, I have found it is more profitable to remain silent."

"But you saved my life and—"

She took Mina away from anyone who could eavesdrop

on their conversation. "No one can know. For reasons I cannot explain."

"No one?"

"Except my father." She leaned closer, allowing Mina this one nibble. "Should he wish it, he can explain."

"It appears that you and I both have secrets we do not want to share."

She searched Mina's tired eyes. "And are you in trouble?"

"Nothing so dangerous. You, on the other hand—"

"I can take care of myself."

"I pray you are right. But in my short lifetime, I have learned that a woman is limited in the type of care she can provide for herself."

"I'm forced to agree." Lora studied Mina, wondering not for the first time what ordeal terrified her so. "I am fortunate. After my mother's death, my father raised me alongside my brother to face obstacles no matter the danger."

"Your father seems too good to be true," Mina said. "Though I dare say some troubles cannot be fought alone."

"I assure you, his ideals are well-founded. Though his passion for life is not what it once was."

Mina's eyes glistened with unshed tears. "Grief is inescapable."

Lora peered over Mina's shoulder to check how the duke and her cousin were getting on. "We must talk further. Until then, trust me. I have not asked about what you are running from. I had only known you minutes before I knew you were truly good. All I ask is that you extend that same faith in me. Believe that I know what is best, at least in this instance."

"But have the terrible things you've accomplished hardened your heart?"

"A woman must know her place," Aunt Meg said as she approached to observe the growing spectacle the duke and

Samuel created. "It is not for us to interfere with the games these men play."

"Aunt!" Her chastisement was quickly shut down.

"Shhh, niece. Something is happening, and I for one am eager to hear."

They moved closer, arm in arm.

"Challenging a man you barely know is a risky business." The duke strapped on a wrist guard, ending his silence. "The target. Dead center hits only."

"Dead center, it is."

"What do you intend to wager, Lieutenant?"

"You assume that I have not done my due diligence, Your Grace," Samuel murmured, his words loaded with ridicule.

"You're mistaken." Beresford selected a bow and tested the string, nocking an arrow. "I know exactly who I'm dealing with and I accept your challenge."

Her cousin's laugh was triumphant. "And the wager?"

"You have only to name it," the duke said sharply. "The choice is yours."

"Aha! Then I offer the kiss of my fair cousin."

Lora blinked, unhappy to be put on the spot. Aunt Meg let out a huff, forcing her cane into the earth. Eliza drew close, clasping Lora's upper arm. Mina moaned her misgivings. The crowd gasped while men lengthened the distance between the two targets to one-hundred paces.

"I'll be the envy of you all when I get to kiss our hostess."

Several guffaws sounded before drifting away in the breeze.

"You forget yourself, nephew," Meg said sternly. "Lady Lora is a human being, not a sack of coin to slap down on a tabletop willy nilly."

The duke stood his ground, unwittingly subjecting Lora to scrutiny. "I accept."

Lora staggered. Were both of them daft? Why, her lips

were not theirs to barter, to be auctioned off to the highest bidder.

Oh, Samuel had hatched foul business; foul business, indeed.

She placed her hand over her mouth to fend off a bout of nausea, uncertain how to bear the shame. Kissing a man publicly was positively scandalous. On the other hand, . . . *No, no, no.* She refused to even consider it. But against her will her mind wandered to the place she dared not go. What would the duke's lips feel like against hers, taste like? *Oof!* Worse. What if she had to kiss her cousin?

Balderdash!

Beresford's high rank made him the perfect match for a marquess's daughter. And she loved him. Oh, how she had always loved him. But she was not in the market for a husband. Marriage would quickly put a stop to her nightly forays into the wilds of Kingston, which was something she could not allow. Nor could she afford a scandal that would see the deed done. The world balanced on her shoulders— the future of the market town, Papa's legacy, stopping Nicholas's killer, and ridding the village of greedy thieves who were not above committing murder. One was still at large and possibly committing injurious crimes, the black-guard she'd encountered on the London Road not surviving.

Her duplicity in that death had shocked her to her bones, so she refused to think about it further. But what if her cousin won? He had a penchant for gambling, winning, and losing with the roll of the dice. She must never underesti-mate him. He was indomitable in his quest to inherit her father's title, Winterbourne, and her.

Good God, was that his purpose? To win and announce his intentions to all and sundry this very day, and before her father lay in his grave?

"You may do the honors, Your Grace." Her cousin's words were biting.

"After you," the duke countered.

Though Samuel looked handsome in his regimentals, she sensed a hint of nervousness in his actions—the flick of a finger—as he positioned himself, drawing back to shoot the first volley. He pulled the bowstring, stretching it taut then, on an exhale, loosed his arrow.

Lora watched with bated breath, daring the projectile to miss. The arrow disappeared into a ray of sunshine with a whoosh, then penetrated the target, missing the bullseye by an eighth of an inch.

Spectators gathered and broke into applause. Samuel smirked, disgruntled but satisfied. He left his post and made a show of straightening the high collar of his uniform as Lora's father limped into sight.

"What do you make of this?" Mina asked. "Do you think the duke can best him?"

"A bluff surely," Lora said. "I have never known my cousin to excel at any sport. His passions have always lent themselves to the gaming tables."

"Your father has arrived." Eliza gave Lora's arm a light squeeze. "Maybe he will put an end to this."

"I do not see how. Beresford agreed to this travesty."

Mina regarded the scene, nodding. "The duke must know something we do not. He *is* older, wiser, more experienced. His physique lends itself to the outdoors. Who's to say?"

Papa hobbled forward and said something to the duke, who looked directly at Lora. Though their eyes met briefly, the tug in her heart pulled as tautly as the bowstring he placed between his fingers.

"Oh, I cannot look," Mina said. "What, do you suppose, did your father say to him? It is obvious he has not stopped the match. The duke is preparing to shoot."

Yes, he was. Every formidable inch of him attracted her like a writhing worm to a fish dangling just out of reach. He moved with grace, nocked his arrow, and drew it back—arms flexing, muscles straining, jaw tense. Then, in one fluid movement, a delicate dance that held her spellbound, his fingers flexed and the shaft let loose.

Those gathered around stared in wonder as his arrow traveled twenty, fifty, eighty to one-hundred yards. *Magnificent arc!* The suspense lingered for what seemed like hours until the tip imbedded dead center on the board.

"Bravo!" several gentlemen shouted to great applause.

"Lora!"

Turning, she came face-to-face with her father.

"It is up to you whether you honor this bet," he said. "No one will say a word if you choose otherwise. I am told you had no part in it, and the duke holds himself to a higher standard than your cousin. Take into consideration that winning a bet is more important to Samuel than your reputation."

"I must go, Lora," Mina said as if desiring to avoid a quarrel. "Ruth is waiting. I fear I have left her alone too long as it is." Mina squeezed her hand reassuringly then withdrew to the house.

"Miss Parr," Papa said, stopping her. Lora watched the pair closely as her father joined Mina. "Please understand, my nephew has been away for several years. Though that does not excuse his inappropriate behavior. I hope it has no bearing on how you view others at Winterbourne."

"Indeed, it does not, my lord."

"Good. I am glad." He offered his arm in a rare, touching tribute. "Allow me to escort you back to the house, then. I understand you enjoy reading, Miss Parr. As it happens, I have just received a first edition of—"

As his voice faded with their retreat, Eliza broke into Lora's thoughts. "Is that not encouraging?"

Watching the pair depart, she asked, "What?"

"The attention your father is giving Miss Parr."

"Yes. Very." She smiled, her heart warming to the lively change in her father's attitude. "And I'm not above wishing Samuel would turn into a frog so that he cannot become master of Winterbourne and the next Marquess of Putney. I am quite piqued that he recklessly gambled my lips away."

"There are worse things to suffer," Eliza said with a sigh.

Her stomach knotted, and she stiffened. "Like what?"

"Being known as a wallflower all of your days."

"Eliza, someday a man will enchant you, and all the years you've spent yearning for that moment will vanish."

The duke divested himself of his bow and the wrist guard, then rubbed the back of his hand across his mouth. Smothering a groan, Lora knew it was unlikely that she would ever forget this mad lurching of her heart whenever she looked at him. She flattened her palms against her dress and watched the duke accept congratulations from those in his vicinity while Samuel stalked up to the house, casting worrisome glances at the woods.

"Don't look now." Lora tore her gaze away from Samuel, reservations about his behavior sinking into the pit of her belly. Why was he so on edge, so desperate to win a bet? "His Grace is heading this way," Eliza whispered, her warning too persuasive to ignore. "I wonder what he will say to you, now that he has won a kiss. Do you suppose he plans to collect his prize?"

"I do not know." Rather, she wasn't sure she wanted to know. It was all so scandalous and stimulating and seductive. A delightful shiver ran through her, warring with her anxiety.

"I have seen the way you look at each other. And do not tell me you feel nothing for him."

"I feel—" Though she was delighted to see her father

finally show interest in living again, she was angry at Samuel. He'd humiliated her, mocked her. And the duke . . . he . . .

"You have done nothing wrong, sweet friend. You are above reproach."

But that wasn't true. She hunted down men and made them pay for their crimes. "I wish Nicholas was here. He'd tell me—" She stopped short in dismay. "Why can't things be different?"

"Because they aren't."

Eliza had a pure heart and, therefore, couldn't possibly understand the dilemma Lora faced. "I am in imminent danger," she said fearful of what the future had in store. "I feel it deep in my bones."

"No," Eliza said, "you are saved."

If only that were true. "Am I?"

"Yes. And now I must venture indoors before I'm christened like a baker. Heaven knows I have enough freckles already. Besides, it's time to face the duke."

"Don't go." She hung on until their hands nearly parted, forcing Eliza to stay.

The duke arrived, his eyes brimming with tenderness and passion, stealing her breath. "My apologies for entertaining that bet, ladies. I had no choice but to defend Lady Lora's honor."

She found her tongue. "I do not need a protector, Your Grace."

"Except that isn't so. Is it?"

She and Eliza exchanged glances, Eliza's eyes imploring her to go along with everything she said. "Your Grace, please allow me to applaud your archery skills. They make my paltry attempts to use a bow pale in comparison."

"No one becomes a proficient without practice, Lady Eliza."

"Thank you for saying so, but that is the problem. I

cannot practice while I am at Winterbourne because Lora doesn't know how to hold a bow."

"Eliza." She blinked back surprise. Why was her friend acting out of character? It benefited no one, especially Lora. If the duke discovered her proficiency with the weapon, he might be led to suspect she was the highwaywoman he'd seen in the woods.

"You see? She's too humble by half. May I prevail upon you to give her a lesson or two? A bit of practice would put us on more equal footing."

Beresford bowed. "I would be honored."

"You see, Lora, we are saved."

"Would you like a lesson today, Lady Lora?" he asked with a faint glint of humor in his eyes. "I am at my leisure."

Eliza put her hand to her forehead, nearly unsettling her bonnet. "Oh, yes, the sooner, the better. But you must excuse me, I am quite famished. Sport kicks up quite the appetite, does it not?"

Lora shot her a warning glare.

"Enjoy your lesson. I shall be over there, chaperoning by the refreshment table. I am quite certain that Lora will be the goddess of the hunt in no time at all."

Some of Lora's frustration evaporated. "Eliza."

"Allow me." Beresford offered his hand. The charge of unbidden energy that shot through her extremities at the contact as he led her to the bow stand, proved this was a bad idea. Once there, he began removing the glove on her right hand, one delicious finger at a time. Her knees weakened, her pulse quickening. He replaced the glove with the wrist guard and began lacing it with slow, infuriating skill. Then, he plucked a bow from the table and stepped behind her, lowering the circumference of it over her head. Heat flushed over her as he whispered close to her ear. "This puts me in mind of Cruikshank's Comic Alphabet."

"A is the archer who shot at a frog," she found herself saying.

"You know it?" he asked, placing her fingers on the string one at a time. "Much can be said of intellectual sport, but there is nothing like having this kind of power in one's hands." How right he was. "It is invigorating. And once a person accepts that power, it flows vicariously through the fingers to the arrow and on to the target. A silky, smooth transition spent on a breath." He eased back her arm, leveling her hand with her cheek. He adjusted her footing and placed his hands on her waist, turning her body toward the target and melting every inhibition she'd been born with. "A line." He flattened his fingers down the length of her left arm, reviving every inch of her until she closed her eyes envisioning their bodies intertwined. "Release."

She leaned into him and turned her head toward his heat, their lips a hairsbreadth apart. Their eyes met for an instant.

"Nock the arrow."

"How?" she asked breathlessly, embracing the theater. "Show me."

The duke cleared his throat and then stiffened suddenly, releasing her arm. Before she knew what had occurred, the bow stand bridged the space between them. "That is enough for today." His gravely tone sounded as if he was in pain, but she had no idea how that could be. He was fine a moment ago. "If you like, we can pick up where we left off tomorrow."

Perplexed, she asked, "Have I done something wrong?"

"No." He shook his head. "Please, excuse me. I just recalled something that requires my immediate attention."

Beresford turned his back and walked away, leaving her staring in his wake.

"Good heavens!" Eliza exclaimed, hurrying to her side. "From where I stood, that was quite entertaining. But what did you say to him? What could have possibly caused an end to your lesson before it began?"

"I hardly know."

Had she given herself away? Did the duke suspect she was the highwaywoman from the woods?

CHAPTER 10

*M*yles kept his distance from Lora for several days, forgoing a picnic, and avoiding her when the ladies strolled about the gardens or passed the time in the estate's massive library. He rose before everyone else to break his fast. He hunted fowl until mid-morning, then handled business into the late afternoon, often meeting one of his men in the woods to receive updates on their activities. Ornate dinners and the occasional musicale arranged by Lora's aunt, Miss Percival, continued to delight guests, and billiards entertained gentlemen over drinks. Even then, however, he could not escape the young woman he'd come to admire and adore. Lora occupied his thoughts, refusing to let go.

Everywhere he went, Lora was there. He saw her face on the surface of the lake. He heard her singing at the pianoforte as the breeze drifted through the trees. She was in his blood, the very breath filling his lungs.

Restless and determined to clear the cobwebbing thoughts clouding his mind, he ordered a horse to be saddled and set out over the green. With everything going on at Darby, and his men being no closer to finding Stuart's killer, desiring Lora seemed wrong. He had a mystery to solve. And rather than school Lora on how to hold a bow, he should be searching for the expert archer—the highwaywoman—who'd shot Grimes. His original goal left no time for dancing or temptation, it required focus. He'd come to Winterbourne to interview the guests, to piece together the puzzle that would paint a broader picture of why the highwaywoman haunted Kingston and Stuart was murdered.

The two were connected. But how?

He revisited the day of the archery tournament in his mind, recalling that he'd only accepted Hawkesbury's challenge to warn off the lieutenant. Her cousin's penchant for gambling and desperation to win was cause for concern. Because of it, he'd been determined to keep Hawkesbury from earning Lora's kiss.

The thought of tasting her soft, dewy lips put him in need of a cold pond.

Who was he trying to fool? A dousing wouldn't cure what ailed him. His instincts about her the night of the Templetons' ball had been precise. Being around Lora and getting to know her only made him desire her more. Her brave spirit, unconquerable heart, and gamble-worthy lips tempted him more than any woman ever had.

If only he could tell her that.

Highly improper.

Wallowing in torment, he took the London Road and headed back to Kingston. His concentration had waned and he needed to recharge. It was Stuart he should be thinking of, plotting and planning to apprehend the ones responsible for his butler's death, not wooing the sensibilities of a good, upstanding woman.

Riding hard, he dismissed the heartache such a decision

triggered, shelving away the losses that catalogued his life. The rakish frivolity in which he'd indulged himself in London prior to his father's death; the duties that he'd immediately thrown himself into and sworn to uphold. Heraldry, honor, and heart. More was the pity. It all paled compared to the spectacled beauty who'd somehow bewitched him, body and soul.

Someone ran out of the trees and dashed across the road in front of him.

To avoid trampling the poor soul, he quickly reined in his mount. The beast reared, and he lost his grip. Grappling for the reins, he fell back and hit the hard earth with a thud. Blinking away the sting to his pride, he slowly rose to his feet, confused.

The moon was full, the woods a mixture of path and shadow. Just as he'd got his wits about him, another figure cloaked in red darted across the road, giving chase to the first.

Gravel crackled beneath his feet as he abandoned his horse and impulsively ran after the two figures, the sound of his approach a stark warning to whoever lurked in the woods. He knew he might be walking into a trap, hemmed in by trees and underbrush with nowhere to run. And yet the desire to discover the identity of the highwaywoman and put an end to his own suffering and that of the inhabitants of Kingston drove him on.

An arrow whooshed through the trees, the whir of a distant warning.

A twig snapped. The resounding strum of the shaft missing its mark and impaling wood followed before the red-clad apparition finally took form. The figure, like that of an avenging huntsman in search of the damned, parted from the trunk of an old oak.

The highwaywoman!

His eyes hadn't deceived him.

The night Stuart died replayed in his head, compelling him to recall seeing her for the first time. Powers of reasoning led him to believe she had not been involved in his butler's death. But she had been there, whether taking part in Stuart's murder or pursuing the killer.

Did she know the killer's identity? Was that who she was after now? If he caught up to her, would she divulge that information willingly?

Burying Stuart had been hard, almost as hard as saying goodbye to his father. The man had been a confidant and friend, family—and Myles had few blood ties left to spare.

Fury seized his good sense, propelling him forward. Tracking was a dangerous sport, especially if you didn't know what or who you were hunting. Nevertheless, he continued to stalk his prey, a rash decision, surely. He was unarmed, but he kept to the trees, aware that her swift and steady aim might instantly seal his doom.

Folklore taught that a wild hunt forebode catastrophe, abduction by fairies or death to the one witnessing it. And like the king of the underworld in Arthurian legend, he meant to make sure that devils—including a certain high-waywoman—did not destroy human souls.

Even if it meant preventing her from capturing and killing the man responsible for Stuart's death?

Justice must prevail. The court passed judgment on a man, no matter the cost to pride or prejudice.

There! A darting to the left.

Her cloak fanned out in dramatic fashion. He moved to outflank his quarry as the figure stretched a bowstring and let another arrow fly. She stilled, her gloved hand hovering over her quiver as she peered through the trees.

Hoping she was distracted by the man's distant cry, he

crept behind her, then stopped dead in his tracks when she said, "Stay where you are." In a split second, he was staring at a nocked bow. "Do not come any closer."

The highwaywoman's voice was husky, strained, as if she altered it to keep from being recognized. "You wouldn't shoot an unarmed man, would you?"

"That depends on the man."

Curious about her identity and who would be revealed beneath the hood, he took a step closer. "I mean you no harm."

"I'm warning you," she said, her voice deepening to a threatening croak. "You shouldn't have followed me. This is none of your concern."

"Everything happening in Kingston concerns me."

"Stay where you are, Your Grace."

The opening Myles waited for had arrived. She knew him, or rather, who he was. Being a duke made that part easy. Raising his hands in mock surrender, he continued to advance slowly, struck by a nagging suspicion that he knew her too. Something about her drew him in, and he sensed that she would not harm him.

She'd allowed Grimes to live, and no one liked a solicitor.

Tightening her bowstring, she eased the arrow back along her cheek. "This arrow isn't meant for you."

"Then don't shoot it," he said matter-of-factly, taking another step.

He didn't get far. Faster than he could blink, the arrow strummed between his feet.

She withdrew another and nocked it, but before she could let loose, he snatched her arm. "Caught you."

Her instincts were sharp. She spun out of reach, outfoxing him. Undeterred, he caught her again. This time, he seized the edge of her cloak, which she quickly shrugged off, moving this way and that through the trees, to evade him. But he was larger, his stride wider and faster. Recapturing the she-devil, he twirled the vixen around in his arms until they came face-to-face.

The shocking collision forced them both to the ground.

"Get off me, you oaf!" she demanded, kicking and squirming and trying to dislodge him. "Let. Me. Go!"

"Hold still," he ordered, trying to process the now familiar voice—

"I can't . . . breathe."

"Lady Lora?" *Impossible!* "Is that you?"

"You big oaf!" She pummeled his arm. "I . . . cannot . . . breathe."

He raised up on his elbows, one eye trained on the direction her arrows loosed, to make sure the wounded man wasn't circling back around to ambush them. "What are you doing here? This is no place for a lady. And why were you wearing a red cloak?"

The questions mounted, but nothing numbed the truth.

Lady Lora is the highwaywoman!

But how could that be? She was a simple wallflower, a modest woman who needed glasses to . . . see.

Stunned by this unbelievable revelation, he glared down at her in annoyance. *Farcical!* The glasses were gone, and she didn't need archery lessons. With deadly precision, she shot her arrows exactly where she wanted them to go.

Anger and frustration radiated off her in waves. Her nostrils flared. "Let. Me. Go," she repeated.

Wild, reckless, irresistible woman. Devil take him, but he couldn't help but admire her derring-do. And when she writhed in his arms, a fiery heat ignited in his loins, making him ache to know her intimately, to feel their bodies glide together in the throes of passion, limbs intertwined. This Lora—this lady—was an aphrodisiac, and he was her pitiful fool. She wasn't a wallflower. She wasn't a female prone to foibles and flaws. She was a tantalizing temptation, a paradox, her complexity sending a shot of desire straight to his loins. The very idea of her intrigued him, making him yearn to sample her charms.

Who would know out in these woods?

He would.

How cleverly she had played him false.

"You are ruining everything!" she shrieked.

Me? "You have done that yourself." Shaking his head in disbelief, he got up, hauling the struggling vixen to his side. "What are you up to? And who are you chasing in the woods?"

"I can explain," she rushed to say.

"I'm listening."

"I know you saw me at your estate. I wanted to tell you then that I didn't kill your man, that I didn't arrive until after someone attacked your butler. But if you want to find the real murderer, the man responsible is getting away."

"Who?"

She stomped her foot with outrage. "The man in the orange neckerchief."

He blinked. "The man—"

"The man who killed my brother!" Her admission pierced his soul. She was chasing the man who murdered the young earl? What kind of foolish fortitude did she possess? "You let him get away!"

Her accusation hit home. Staggering back, he realized he hadn't been there when his father died. He hadn't been in residence when Stuart was murdered. Each time, he hadn't been able to stop Fate, no matter how long he'd fought in the House of Lords to forge his destiny. And by intercepting Lora, he'd hindered the hunt, permitting the true slayer to escape.

Their gazes locked, hers vengeful, his self-loathing and suspicious. In the seconds they stood face-to-face, he recognized her, the real Lady Lora Putney, for the first time. She embodied vengeance, a Fury born from blood and death, the one who could not be escaped. Her previous timidity had hidden mad rage and frenzy, and like Nemesis, she sought retribution for the evil deeds of men, serving portion for due portion to what each man deserved.

How did she do it? What source offered the kind of courage required to do what she'd done? And how long did she expect to keep up pretenses without succumbing to the same sins as the outlaws she hunted?

"You are after your brother's killer?" he asked, dumbfounded.

"Killers," she said coldly, the ice in her tone chilling him to the bone. "One provided the death blow, the other the order. And now, the man I saw kill my brother with my own eyes is gone because you allowed him to get away!"

She moved to leave, but he stopped her. "You are going to get yourself killed."

"It doesn't matter. I died one year ago. Now, let me go," she pleaded. "He's getting away."

Her daring brown eyes reflected moonlight, the glittering orbs reeling him in like the siren who lured Odysseus. He'd misjudged her. She was not plain and unaccomplished. She was anything but.

"I will explain, but not now." A healthy blush colored her cheeks. "You have my word. Only, let me go."

She expected him to believe her? "You have done nothing but lie to me from the moment we met."

"I can say the same about you, Your Grace."

She was right. She'd used him, he suspected, to get back at her cousin, and he'd used her to gain access to her father. Checkmate.

"We have much to discuss."

"We do." She bit her lower lip, a devious and delicious temptation, reminding him of the kiss he'd won and had yet to collect. He was at a crossroads. While he yearned to crush her in his arms and kiss away her crazed ambitions, he also needed to stop her fool's errand. They couldn't accomplish anything in the dark. Didn't she know that? "Another time, however."

What if she dashes off and gets herself killed?

He retrieved her cloak and handed it to her, watching closely as she fastened the clasp at the hollow below her chin. "I cannot let you chase after a murderer alone. Surely, you cannot expect that of me? I am a gentleman and, therefore, must offer my protection. Allow me to accompany you."

"That is . . . a fine suggestion, but you will only—"

"Slow you down." He comprehended her meaning and her limited belief in his abilities cut him to the quick. But, he conceded, the man she'd wounded had a head start, and the odds were against either of them catching him now. There was no reason to hamstring her with his presence. He'd seen her in action and knew exactly what she could do. "Meet me privately, then."

She hesitantly agreed. "There is a bothy near the old farmhouse located behind the folly on my estate."

"I will find it."

She raised her hood. "Meet me there in two hours."

Their gazes locked and then she slipped away, disappearing into the woods like a wraith melting into shadow.

Myles stood still for several moments, listening to the night and trying to process what he'd just learned.

An owl hooted a warning, and something scurried off in the trees, making him wonder if the legends of hell-hounds were true. Reality was strange. Never in his wildest dreams could he have imagined that Lady Lora was the avenging highwaywoman.

Who then was targeting Kingston? And what was this hold Lora had on him whenever she was near?

Maddened by these unanswered questions, he strode out of the woods and located his horse without too much difficulty. It had been trained to stay close and not wander far. Unfortunately, he couldn't say the same thing about his thoughts. He'd always believed that a man could do anything with the right information. And what better way to assess the quicksand before him than to ride back to Winterbourne and locate that farmhouse.

Lady Lora is no wallflower. But her quest for vengeance might do more than wilt her resolve.

What was a man supposed to do with that information?

Questioning his own motives, he took the trail back to Winterbourne, locating the farmhouse easily enough after having studied a map of the estate before arriving to question Putney. Hidden by the folly and an alcove of trees, the small bothy paled in comparison to the main house and the immense size of the estate. Tying his horse's reins to a branch, he carefully opened the door and went inside and waited.

Surprisingly, Lora was true to her word. When she joined him an hour later, she looked defeated. "He got away."

The agony in her voice as she lowered her bow and quiver to the fireside table, and removed her cloak, made him squirm. She wore men's breeches and a corset over a loose linen shirt, her shapely form one he'd never forget. He struggled to think and fought for the right words. "How long have you been chasing the man in the orange neckerchief?"

"Almost a year."

Since the young earl's death. "What happened to your brother?"

She sat down and glanced out the lodge window, smiling sadly. "We were racing on the downs. I allowed Nicholas to win, of course, which put him ahead of me by one horse length. Tempted as I was to race ahead, maybe I could have prevented his death."

In that case, he might never have met her. "Your brother's death isn't the work of a random thief. I suspect that no matter how far ahead of him you were, he was the intended target."

Locked in her memories, she must not have heard him.

"It all happened so fast," she said. "I saw Nicholas fall. He hit the ground and there was nothing I could do to stop it. Nothing whatsoever. By the time I reached him, he was gone."

He understood her agony better than she knew. Stuart's death stare flashed before his own eyes.

"My world ended that day. I didn't know what to do, where to go. How to tell my father. Until I saw *him*."

"The man with the orange neckerchief?"

She clenched her jaw, nodding. "He . . . taunted me. Threatened to kill me, too. That moment still haunts my dreams." She rose unsteadily to her feet. He rushed to her side when it appeared she might collapse from sheer exhaustion. She shooed him away. "I swore then that I would get my revenge. But there's more. Someone sent him here."

"How do you know this?"

"His partner was attacking Miss Parr and Miss Finch on the London Road several nights ago. When I discovered them, the poor dears were frightened half to death. And after . . . after what I suspect the man in the orange neckerchief did to your butler, I—" She started to shake. He stepped forward, and she walked into his arms. "This can't go on. I cannot keep—"

"You do not have to do this alone. I am here," he assured

her, tightening his embrace. "Dark forces are at work, but we will outwit them together."

"What do you mean?"

He rubbed his chin against her braided hair, inhaling her scent—leather and horse and a hint of violets. "Who stands to gain from your father and brother's deaths?"

"My uncle is next in line." She tilted her head back to stare up at him. "If you are suggesting that he would purposefully harm my most beloved brother, you could not be more wrong." Shaking her head as if reluctantly working through the possibility that her uncle had deceived them, she broke away. "No," she said.

He felt her rejection of his suggestion keenly.

"I do not believe it. I will not. Moreover, my uncle is not well. Dr. Wells told me he's developed an odd cough, and, at times, seems to be in a stupor, though he's never taken sick a day in his life. It is relieving to know that Dr. Wells sent a servant to procure an elixir for what ails my uncle." She stopped pacing, as if processing what she'd just told him. "My cousin, Samuel, however, is my uncle's heir. If anything happened to my uncle—" She strode to the window, peering out. "As much as I loathe my cousin, his taunts and persistent gambling, the truth is I cannot lay the blame at his feet. He has been with his regiment."

"Has he?" If the papers in Grimes's possession were any indication, Hawkesbury had been investigating his own son. The reports from Jonathan 'Jew' King, Howard and Gibbs, and King's Hamlet's could explain why. London moneylenders were notorious for refusing to forgive debts. "Evil has a way of seeping under the securest doors."

She whirled to face him. "What do you mean?"

"Samuel could have hired men to do his bidding."

"With what? He's gambled any blunt he's had away. No."

Her wretched expression lanced him. "My father and uncle would have to die before Samuel receives another farthing."

"The plan, surely," he suggested. From her shocked expression, Lora had not considered such a betrayal. He pressed on. "Think on it. Your father suffered an unlikely hunting accident. How?"

"The girth strap on his saddle failed."

"I see. Someone murdered your brother."

"I just told you that." Her eyes narrowed. "By a man in an orange neckerchief."

"Who stands in the way of your cousin inheriting Winterbourne?"

"Papa and my uncle."

"And your cousin just returned from the Continent and your uncle has conveniently become ill." As he aired the facts —he suspected, confirming her fears—the tension in the old lodge thickened. "Doesn't that seem suspicious to you?"

Anger lit her eyes. "Samuel is many things, but he is not a killer. He prefers to prolong his cruelty."

"Reckless gambling can make good men do horrible things."

She stiffened. "He has been acting strangely lately, as if he is afraid of his own shadow."

"Moneylenders employ men who often take matters into their own hands. Is it possible your cousin intends to liquidate the estate to pay off his debts? If that is the case, maybe they sought to speed up his inheritance by killing your brother and poisoning your uncle."

She gasped and he drew her into his embrace. "Do you think someone poisoned my uncle?"

"The signs are there—the cough, the stupor, and instability. I almost saw him collapse the night of the ball."

She tilted her head back to look up at him, blinking back bafflement.

"Perhaps we should bring this to your father's attention. He has been kept in the dark for far too long, don't you agree?"

"I've been trying to protect him."

"You cannot shield him from the truth or keep dashing off into danger, Lora. The longer you deny your cousin what he considers to be his birthright and the longer he owes dangerous people money, the more crazed and unpredictable he will become."

"I cannot involve my father. He's lost so much." She abandoned his arms and moved to the table. There, she picked up the red cloak and held it up to her nose, inhaling its scent. "This is all I have left of Nicholas. All I know how to do. Without revenge, I am nothing but a wallflower waiting to be asked to dance."

"You are not shy and silent, Lora. You are bold and beautiful and brave."

"That is not the impression you left me with three years ago at the Templetons' ball. You danced with everyone else in the room but me."

Bollocks! She remembered.

"What would you say if I told you that I didn't ask you to dance because I found you attractive? Don't turn away, I am being honest. Doting mamas and eager young ladies surrounded me on all sides. It was a Herculean effort just to speak to my fellows. I had no intention of forming an attachment. Love would have impeded my scholarly pursuits." He reached out to caress her cheek, wiping away an errant tear. "Lady Vengeance, you have carried this burden alone for too long. Forget the past—my mistakes, the horrors you've faced. I am here. Now. Standing before you as a man besotted, offering my help and pleading for you to take care with my heart." Lowering his forehead to hers, he whispered, "Dance with me?"

The silence became deafening as he waited for her to acknowledge that he'd unlocked his soul and heart.

"You are daft. There isn't any music."

"Then we shall make our own." He raised her chin gently, his spirits soaring, coaxing her to meet his gaze. "From the moment you beguiled me at the Templetons' ball—patience and propriety your only weapons—I have wanted only you." *To kiss the pulsing beat at the base of your throat and feel your heartbeat thud against mine.* But he couldn't tell her that now. Nothing could make up for the years he'd allowed to pass unchecked, or the heartbreak she'd endured alone. "Despite everything—outside threats— the courage you have shown to right wrongs, and the losses we have both experienced, you still make me want to be better, stronger, cleverer. If I could, I would strut about like a peacock to win your heart."

"That would be a sight, wouldn't it?"

"It would be the start of many things." He ran his finger along her jaw.

"What kinds of things?"

He peered at her intently. "This." He kissed her forehead. "This." He kissed the tip of her nose. "And this." The moment their lips met, the ground fell away. "Now," he said, hardly recognizing his voice. "Imagine that, but all over."

Her eyes widened. "All o—"

"Everywhere."

"Show me," she said, her breath as light as a sigh.

"Now?" he asked, slipping his hands over her arms. "What about your plan to catch the man in the orange neckerchief?"

"I have not been able to catch him for a year and I am tired of chasing ghosts. I am weary of this heartache and long for the good in this world. I need assurance that my life is not doomed. Show me there is more than death and deceit, tears and torment. I fear if I do not experience love now, I never shall."

"*Fortune and love favor the brave.*'" He pulled her to him, whispering in her ear. "And you have been fearless for far too long."

"Show me," she whispered, her breath fanning his face.

Driven mad by need and desire, he could hardly resist her invitation. If he lost her, he would never find her equal again. She deserved to be loved, to know that the rest of her days would be filled with joy and happiness. "Are you sure this is what you want? Once you cross this threshold, there will be no turning back. You will be mine, and I yours."

She relaxed into his embrace. "Haven't we always been?"

He chuckled. "I guess you are right." Indeed, instinct diverted him to years of caprice, which he regretted whole-heartedly. The young woman she was then, however, was not the wild, untamed creature in his possession now.

No man walked away from such a woman.

"A look across a ballroom floor. Secret yearnings and public partings." She pressed her lips to his, giving him his prize. The heady sensation increased his desire. "I never set out to be a wallflower. Yet, after I saw you, no one else could compare. Even when life thwarted plans for another season, I knew we were destined for each other. My aunt, good soul, has always been a wallflower. She instructed me to seize happiness when it comes, no matter the cost, the sacrifice."

"You have sacrificed more than anyone I know."

"Whatever happens, Your Grace." She brushed a lock of hair out of his eyes. "Do not let me become her."

"Perhaps to start," he suggested, "you should call me Myles."

"Myles." Her voice was a soft entreaty that touched his soul. "Promise me. I want love, marriage, children."

"I promise." He crushed her to him, filled with a burning desire and an aching need to soften her hurt and make her his. As he roused her passions, his determination to be everything she needed grew stronger. Dipping into divine ecstasy and buffeted by savage hunger, hope sang in his veins. "Lora. Let me love you."

But would love be enough to help them put the past behind them?

CHAPTER 11

*S*everal days later, no one was surprised by the costumed figures posturing in the halls: lofty characters and low samples of foolery, old women, shepherdesses, sultanas, gypsies, kings, queens, chimney sweeps, sailors, Spaniards and Turks, all eager to participate in a masquerade. The highly anticipated event, a sort of blind-mans-bluff, had the entire household—both guests and servants alike—humming with excitement. Stage oddities moved from one room to another, two-by-two. Eclipsed faces protected secrets, and half masks and Harlequins were worn so close as to make it almost impossible to guess whether one was male or female. In addition to the fictitious transport, fumes of port and palatable wines, and cheerful laughter made clear that pleasure was found, and the orders received from masque warehouses in Town met with approval.

Tonight, Mrs. Management—Aunt Meg, posing as Hestia, the goddess of hearth and home—led the young and dissolute with revelry, turning propriety and sobriety on their heads. Meaner than bad theater, a hazard to virtue and innocence, a Venetian ridotto saved decency and behavioral license for the grand disclosure after supper.

For her part, Lora, garbed as a domino in a half-mask, took in the splendor with a heavy heart. Well-heeled Harlequins marched past, along with country parsons paired with unconventional nuns, and characters of Fortune who baited mythical gods.

An old crone leaning heavily on a cane got support from an Indian maiden. After years of tending to her father's infirmity, Lora recognized his unique gait. Her father's comical performance earned him a smile, while sympathy from said maiden—Mina—made him snicker. She was growing quite fond of Mina and her reviving nature. Though she had still to reveal what it was, in particular, that she was running from, it was plain that she was falling in love with Lora's father as they bonded over books and ballads. Ruth, her maid, was never far. Even now, she skulked about like a sentinel prepared to order one's doom.

Lora sincerely hoped Fortune smiled upon her father and Mina. Marriage might produce the heir that Papa so desperately desired, ruining Samuel's nefarious campaign.

Thinking of her cousin brought her up short. She spotted him almost immediately, dressed appropriately like a red devil and prepared to wreak havoc on innocent lives. His strange secrecy, outstanding gambling debts, and associations with moneylenders resulted in a disastrous combination. As such, the profusion of jewels and elegant dress flamboyantly displayed about them were tempting morsels for nimble digits.

Take the bait.

"Come one, come all," a gypsy cried as musicians struck up a waltz.

Would their quarry, Clyde, risk an appearance?

"Should we go over the plan one more time?" Myles

asked, sweeping her into the Viennese waltz. In contrast, he wore muddied, tattered clothes like a peasant, the exact opposite of refinement and grace, and they shared a rare moment of emotion. "It's not too late to change your mind."

She hardly knew where this nightmare had begun or how it would end. She owed it to herself, to Papa and her sick uncle, to Aunt Meg and Mina and Eliza to see this through. Whatever that end might be. "If Samuel doesn't—"

"He will not pass up the chance to pay off his debts. Mark my words."

She smiled at her peasant, recalling the straw she'd picked out of his hair after their sensual interlude in the bothy. "I'd rather taste your lips again."

"I can arrange that," he said, spinning her around to avoid a jester attempting to identify them. "But not yet."

"Do you think anyone knows that I am your domino?"

"You will never be my domino. You are my Artemis." The red devil appeared, weaving through the crowded room. Lora caught sight of him out of the corner of her eye. Myles must have seen him too, because he said, "It's time."

They parted, separating slowly like ships in the night, tacking starboard and portside, Myles going right and Lora taking the left.

"Remember. You will never be alone," he'd told her in the wee hours of the morning. *"My men are all over the estate and prepared to protect you and your family, regardless of the price to be paid. If we are to put a stop to this madness, we must get your cousin to confess."*

The plan was sound. She had to trust it.

She wove her way through the crush as the Viennese Waltz ended, brushing past a woman in Elizabethan dress who began to sing an ode to victory over the French, the novelty putting everyone in good humor. Laughing gaily to fit in, she knew that foreign influence mattered little to their guests. Masquerades were Venetian in nature. The appeal loosened the harness of ceremony and form, gambling and music, and rewarded pleasure over deprivation. And happy voices signaled that the *fête* was off to a good start.

Indeed, Winterbourne had miraculously come to life. Dancers waltzed over the parquet floor, their disguises illuminated beneath gleaming candelabras and wall sconces that heated up the space. Beeswax and lemon hinted a tremendous amount of work had gone into preparing for the masque. And Aunt Meg had arranged for footmen to open the veranda doors late into the evening, the idea being to draw the eye outward to lighted garden paths, an invitation to anyone with a taste for adventure and a desire for fresh air. The open area also enabled guests to slip in unnoticed or easily escape—like her cousin.

Samuel, where are you?

There.

A pair of devil's horns skirted the crowded room then paused before picking up the cadence once more. Curious, Lora trailed him. Footmen poured spirits into glasses all around her. The clink of crystal, the merriment, the avarice, the speed with which her cousin pillaged unsuspecting women of priceless gems made her dizzy.

The pattern continued for nigh on twenty minutes until everything became clear. Samuel had resorted to thievery to pay off his creditors. If she hadn't witnessed the devilry for herself, she never would have imagined it possible.

A Hawkesbury driven to steal. The very idea!

The surname itself meant 'deep water.' How far into the abyss was Samuel willing to sink in order to become the next Marquess of Putney? Worse. Had he poisoned his own father to get him out of the line of succession, as Myles had suggested?

She crept closer, distrust blackening her mind, as Samuel

seduced yet another oblivious woman. He whispered something near the poor girl's nape before plucking a necklace from her heavily endowed bosom and swiftly stowing the accoutrement under his double-breasted coat before anyone was the wiser. Like a city pickpocket, the entire process took seconds, leaving the social butterfly purring with sublime ecstasy.

Samuel was skilled at this. He had done this before!

Feathers bobbed and turbans dipped as courtesies were exchanged, signaling the start of another waltz. Several bars later, the floor undulated with expectancy, and in the excitement, she lost sight of Myles. She chewed her bottom lip, unsure how to proceed. If she did not follow Samuel through the veranda doors, he, too, would be out of reach if she waited for the duke.

Lowering the hood of her cloak over her forehead, she quickly decided to follow her cousin, but before she could pass the threshold, someone grabbed her arm. Myles? "He is leaving," she said, thinking he'd come to fetch her.

"Who?" Not Myles. Eliza, dressed as a *belle Parisienne*. "Where are you going?"

Lora spun around at the sound of Eliza's voice. "I don't have time to explain. I must go quickly."

"Where?" she asked as Lora searched the gardens. "Never mind, I shall go with you. It isn't safe to be unchaperoned at night."

"Thank you," she said, desiring to keep her friend safe, "but I must do this on my own. There is one thing you can do for me, however."

"What?" Eliza asked. "Are you in any kind of trouble? Has your cousin upset you? A masque is supposed to be a comedy of errors. People pretending to be someone else. Surely—"

"It is Samuel," Lora said, allowing the reference to sink in.

"Yes, indeed. He's gone into the gardens and I must follow him there."

"I cannot allow you to chase after Hawkesbury alone."

"You must." She squeezed Eliza's hand. "Find the duke. It is terribly important that you do. Tell him . . . tell him, *'No man means evil but the devil, and we shall know him by his horns.'*"

"But where?"

She didn't give Eliza time to argue. Dropping her hand, she slipped out onto the veranda and into the garden. The paths were well-lit, Meg's way of lessening the promiscuity when beaux forgot their sporting wit and belles their studied repartees.

Samuel had a head start, forcing her to rely on instinct, which told her that whoever Samuel was hastening to meet would not want witnesses. That increased the danger. Staying aware, she made her way through manicured hedges, taking an opening into another section of the garden, this one far removed from the main house. There, for an instant, she caught sight of a retreating red cape. Darting in that direction, she rounded the hedgerow only to have her arm grabbed from behind and a sharp knife put to her throat.

"Ye don't give up, do ye?"

"Clyde, I presume," she said, struggling to keep her throat as far away from the blade as possible.

"Don't hurt her," Samuel spat as he emerged from the bushes, waving his arms in the air and producing the pouch of stolen articles. "I brought what you demanded." He tossed the bag at Clyde's feet. It landed with a jingle on the thick grass.

"Take it and go. Inform the Jew King that I have settled my debts."

"Ye're daft. I'll take the lot, and 'er, too, fer me trouble." Clyde grimaced as she strained against him, then stopped when the dagger pierced her skin. "Else she takes 'er revenge out on me and I'm set before Captain Tom to go up the ladder to me bed."

"What do you mean?" Samuel asked, paling at the sight of blood trickling down her throat. "All you have to do is take the jewels and money and go."

"*This* is why." He jerked Lora around to face him. "Don't ye know who she is? She's the highwaywoman."

"Lora?" Samuel grinned. "You jest, surely. My cousin could not harm a fly. Why, she can't even shoot a bow."

"Are ye daft? Look at her hooded cloak."

"It's a domino costume."

"She *can* wield a bow. I've seen it. She 'unted with 'er brother and shot me in the back."

Intense astonishment covered Samuel's face. "But she—"

"Tricked ye. Argh. I should 'ave cut 'er down along with 'er brother, but ye bade me not to. I was a fool to listen to ye. She's been a thorn in me side ever since."

"What did you say?" Lora asked, fire burning in her belly.

"Ye 'eard that right." Clyde cackled gleefully. "Yer cousin ordered me to kill the earl."

"That isn't how it happened." The hollow denial flew from Samuel like a lightning bolt. "Don't believe him. He—"

"I will kill you for this!" The betrayal blinded her. She bucked and clenched her teeth, so furious she could barely speak.

"Ye see?" He yanked her closer, the blade pricking deeper than before. "Not so tame, after all. If only ye'd known this sooner, 'Awkesbury. Mayhap then I could 'ave saved ye the trouble of 'avin' to kill 'er now."

"Don't kill her," Samuel cried. He threw off his devil horns and reached out the palm of his hand as if to calm Clyde. "She's no good to me dead."

"I can't let 'er go. She knows too much. She'll be the death of us."

"No! No, she won't," Samuel reasoned. "Tell him, Lora. Agree to call off this vendetta of yours. I have a plan. It demands sacrifices, but when I inherit, we can marry. The two of us will have everything."

"Not my brother, and certainly not my father and uncle, who will have to die before your delirious dream comes to fruition. If you think for one moment that I would ever marry you after what you've done, and what I suspect you've done to your own father—"

"Poisonin' 'is father was easy. Got a maid to think she was bein' 'elpful with a tonic fer the master. 'Awkesbury, 'ere, can't get 'is 'ands dirty, ye see. Why, even 'is uniform is borrowed. 33rd Regiment of Foot, my arse. If e'd been to France, e'd have one of Wellington's medals and 'e'd be carryin' it round, country-put."

Samuel must be a silly nube in order to have agreed to such degenerate behavior.

"But the dog booby faked 'is conscription and flashed it off 'alf seas over, usin' the blunt fer 'is commission to go a whorin' and gamblin' in Town, while me and me mate made it look like Kingston 'ad a problem with bandits. 'Twas the only way to keep Jack in 'is office."

Shock yielded quickly to fury. "You killed the duke's butler?"

"Aye. The old sot wrestled me to the end."

"Shut it!" Samuel shouted. "You're ruining everything!"

"Quit bein' a Spanish trumpeter. Ye forget I 'eard ye promise the Jew King ye'd be the next marquess, me lad."

Lora grabbed Clyde's hand to shove the tip of the dagger away from her neck. She had known Samuel was depraved, but she had never suspected the extent of his wickedness. "You despicable—"

"A debt unpaid is a life enslaved. 'E'll never cut even now. And so, it's time to tell yer pretty bird goodbye." Clyde lifted his hand, angling the blade against Lora's neck.

"Stop!" Samuel shouted.

"She'll never marry ye now, 'Awkesbury."

Lora took advantage of the distraction. She grabbed Clyde's arm, shoved the blade away from her neck, stomped on his foot, and then elbowed him in the ribs. Clyde's howl of pain confirmed, as she broke free, that she'd shot him while chasing him off the London Road. Enraged, he lunged for her, but before he could stab her, Samuel stepped in, taking the dagger up to the hilt. He let out a grunt and clutched at his stomach, staggering back, staring at his mid-section in disbelief.

Clyde charged. A searing whoosh whistled by her and a thump split the air before chaos ensued. Men swooped in from every direction, surrounding Clyde, who lay unmoving on the ground with an arrow impaled in his heart, and Samuel, who sank to his knees.

Before she could react, Myles was suddenly there. He dropped a bow and quiver and pulled her into his embrace. "I thought I'd lost you," he said against her ear.

She wrapped her arms around him, staring over his shoulder at the hedges, listening to the voices that blended together all around them. "Did you hear?" she asked, near tears.

"Everything." He withdrew and pulled out a handkerchief, wrapping it around her neck to staunch the trickle of blood still oozing from her wound. "No one will ever harm you or your family again. I'll see to it." He smiled and clutched her hand in his, declaring, "From this moment forward, we shall never be parted."

"What about Samuel?" she asked, trying to hide the faint tremor in her voice.

"Lora."

Samuel's entreaty snatched a piece of her soul. *Blood of the covenant is thicker than water of the womb.* She broke away from Myles, understanding Shakespeare's message, and approached her suffering cousin.

His eyes appeared enlarged and glassy. "Lora."

"I am here." Though she preferred to be anywhere else.

"I don't want to die alone."

"I am here," she repeated. Had he ever bothered to wonder how Nicholas felt the day he died? She bit back despair and took his hand, committed to standing guard and doing the unthinkable—watching the life drain out of his eyes. His undeniable and dreadful duplicity in Nicholas's death cut deep, his betrayal something she would never forget. "I won't let you die alone."

"I am sorry," he blurted out. "Nicholas had everything I wanted, and it . . . altered me. Something snapped inside . . . I couldn't control myself . . ."

"Shhh. Make peace with yourself."

"I cannot," he said, seizing. "I cannot go to my grave . . . knowing . . . you hate me."

She glanced at Myles, understanding the bonds we chose were more significant than the ones provided at birth. Myles loved her, and she loved him. Through all that they'd lost, there was still time to make lasting connections. Papa had found love and wanted to live again. Uncle Thomas was recovering. Aunt Meg would be satisfied knowing that Lora wasn't going to be a spinster. Eliza's future would benefit from Myles's influence.

Slowly, she let go of the heartache, the loss, the pain, and the lady sworn to vengeance. "I forgive you." When she glanced up, she fancied she saw an apparition of Nicholas standing by the hedge. He smiled in that rakish way of his, gave her a nod, and walked into the bushes, disappearing from sight. Swallowing back tears, she looked down at her suffering cousin. "I forgive you, Samuel."

"He's gone," Myles said, lifting her to her feet. "His hold on Winterbourne is over."

Was it? She hardly knew. She moved into Myles's arms, drinking in the comfort of his nearness. "I am sorry."

"What have you to be sorry for? It is I who should apologize to you. If I had just danced with you at the Templetons' ball, perhaps none of this would have happened."

"Don't do that. Don't wish the time we have away." She stared at him with longing. "You are here, now. We have saved each other's lives."

"Indeed, we have." He smoothed her hair and adjusted her cloak. "Have I told you that I love you, Lora?"

"No." She fought tears that refused to fall as the men dispersed and his heart thudded against her own. "Not in so many words."

"Well then." He held her hands and lowered to one knee. "I love you."

"What are you doing?"

"It isn't every day a man falls in love with a wallflower, only to discover that she is the highwaywoman terrorizing the countryside."

"I did nothing of the sort. Get up."

"I want to see what you look like from down here whilst I place you on a pedestal. Be prepared to live at lofty heights for the rest of your days, my love."

Several of the men hauling Samuel's body away chuckled and saluted Myles.

"Your Grace." A delightful shiver washed over her. "Which do you prefer?"

"You." He rose to his feet. "I shall love you in all your incarnations. Lora. Marry me, Lady Vengeance. Make me the happiest of men."

"Yes," she said, nodding and overcome with emotion. "A thousand times, yes."

"Yes?" He grinned. "In that case, I shall worship the ground you walk on for the rest of your days."

"That may be a very long time. Are you prepared?"

His mouth twitched with amusement. "I am."

"Then I must tell you that I love you, Myles. I always have. I always will."

"Brilliant. I shall request a special license straightaway." He placed her hand on his arm and began leading her back through the gardens, where music drifted on the breeze. "Are you ready to return to the masque? I intend to speak to your father."

"Please wait," she said. "That is, let him have his fun." No one could replace Nicholas, but there was contentment in knowing that Papa, that anyone, could start again. "Who knows? If we're lucky, we might have a double wedding."

EPILOGUE

One year later . . .

Winterbourne had weathered the darkest of days—love, loss, betrayal, and rebirth over hundreds of years. In the aftermath of Samuel's deceit, Kingston, Darby, and the rest had received justice. Residents slept more peacefully at night, knowing highwaymen and highwaywomen no longer haunted the London Road, and looked out for one another. And people only referred to the term "wallflower" when describing flora growing along the edges of landscaped gardens.

At Kingston, Lady Eliza surprised everyone by announcing she'd accepted Mr. Stanhope's offer of marriage. The happy couple settled in a roomy cottage at Darby, where the solicitor replaced Clifford Henry and made a living as the Duke of Beresford's current private secretary.

Uncle Thomas's health continued to improve, and the stinging sense that he'd failed his son faded as his brother, the Marquess of Putney, required assistance in business matters.

Aunt Meg was in high demand after the success of the masquerade. She continued to handle Winterbourne's daily affairs, offsetting the burden now facing Papa's new wife, Mina, who'd born a set of twins—a pair of boys. Mina, meanwhile, had unburdened her heart. She had been running away the night Lora rescued her, in order to escape being forced into marriage with a miser three times her age who had a violent disposition. No petition to her father, a baron, ever brought assistance. Though the adventure had nearly cost her life, all was well and good because the situation had led her to Winterbourne and the Marquess of Putney.

Papa's health continued to take a miraculous turn, in part, thanks to Mina's tender loving care and the twins' birth nearly nine months to the day after their nuptials.

But that was not all.

Lora lowered her quill, tired of logging the events in her book. A part of her yearned to ride pell-mell across the downs at a breakneck pace in search of those committing dastardly deeds. That was conduct unbecoming of a duchess, however.

"Put Lady Vengeance away, Lora," Myles demanded, "and come to bed. I have been waiting nearly an hour for a look, a wink, or some sort of loving gesture."

"Very well." She blotted the page and closed the volume, placing the feathered quill back in its stand. Turning in her chair, she tsked. "My poor beloved duke. Who would dare ignore a man of your magnificent stature? Certainly, not I. For I would never resign to leave you holding up a wall."

"The Templetons again. Do you not see that I am sitting with my back against the wall? It is I who am the wallflower now." She smiled, mischievously. "Formidable creature. Gallivanting off hither and yon." He patted the counterpane. "Doing good everywhere but here, where you belong."

"And what services do you require, Your Grace?"

"Pleasure readily comes to mind."

She knelt at the foot of the bed, a hint of a smile curving her luscious lips. "What type of pleasure?"

"Come closer and find out."

"Patience." She stretched out her arm and aimed an imaginary arrow at his heart. "Bullseye."

"Do you miss it?"

"Nocking your bow?" She licked her lips. "I never miss."

"Oh, sweet vengeance, come my way!"

Thank you for reading *LADY VENGEANCE,* Book 24 out of 53 in the Revenge of the Wallflower Series. If you enjoyed Lora and Myles's story, I would be extremely grateful if you left a short review.

And don't forget to purchase all the books in the series.

Revenge is a dish best served cold... Or is it? These wallflowers are about to find out, as they plot against those most deserving. Can society handle a wallflower's revenge? Or will their targets topple one by one?

Revenge of the Wallflowers

ALSO BY KATHERINE BONE

The Nelson's Tea Series

The Nelson's Tea Series is a fast-paced, perilous world of ticking clocks and the clandestine men and women willing to die to protect England and the ones they love.

"Read along as Katherine Bone works her magic in the world of danger, intrigue and spies. You won't be disappointed!!" — Reviewer

My Lord Rogue

Book 1 of 4

Espionage, secrecy, and thwarted assassination attempts. The only thing more dangerous is being in love...

Gillian Chauncey, Baroness Chauncey, is a master of disguise, trained by her expatriated husband, a former French royalist, in the arts of espionage. When a dangerous life or death secret lands in her lap, she's thrust into a perilous world of ticking clocks and desperation, arrowing her directly into the arms of the man who arranged her marriage.

Lord Simon Danbury is no ordinary nobleman. He's been tasked by Admiral Nelson to organize an elite group of clandestine first sons willing to sacrifice all to protect England's shores. When an assassination attempt is made on Nelson, Simon isn't sure what poses more danger, the enemy or the masterfully seductive Gillian.

* * *

The Regent's Revenge Series

Follow the Black Regent's adventures, Cornwall's Robin Hood, a 19th Century pirate portrayed by several men who sail the *Fury* along the coast to rid Southern England of brigands and save damsels in distress.

"Love, secrets, lifelong friends, men of honor and a woman whose husband rises from the ashes to save her." — Reviewer

The Pirate's Duchess

Book 1 of 3

Just when she decided to remarry ...

Duty forces him to take on the pirate code, but honor brings him back.

Prudence, Duchess of Blackmoor, has one desire—to be happy again. After struggling to overcome the horrifying death of her husband, she accepts an earl's offer of marriage, confident she's taking a step in the right direction. But demons, refuse to die, and Prudence finds herself caught in an intricate web of deceit that threatens the very foundations of all she holds dear.

Tobias, the Duke of Blackmoor, crosses the line when an assassination attempt on him fails. To restore the reputations of friends under attack by the same villain, and ensure his wife's safety, he stages his own death, becoming The Black Regent, a notorious pirate bent on brandishing justice, never thinking he'd survive. But to his amazement, he has, and now the darkest-kept secrets are not worth losing the duchess his wife has become.

Find more Katherine Bone books

ABOUT THE AUTHOR

National best-selling historical romance author **Katherine Bone** has been passionate about history since she had the opportunity to travel to various Army bases, castles, battlegrounds, and cathedrals as an Army brat turned officer's wife. Who knew that an Army wife's passion for romance novels would lead to pirates? Certainly not her rogue, whose Alma Mater's adage is "Go Army. Beat Navy!" Now enjoying the best of both worlds, Katherine lives with her rogue in the south where she writes about rogues, rebels, and rakes—aka pirates, lords, captains, duty, honor, and country—and the happily-ever-afters that every alpha male and damsel deserve.

Newsletter
Website

bookbub.com/authors/katherine-bone
facebook.com/AuthorKatherineBone
instagram.com/katlbone
pinterest.com/katlbone
x.com/katherinelbone